For my team:
my husband Whit and my agent Bruce Butterfield.
Thank you for believing in me.
Also for my grandma, "Cookie,"
who continues to be an example to me
of how to nurture friendships over a lifetime.

❧

Check out www.FiftiesChix.com for updates on the Fifties Chix book series, more info on your fave characters, secret diary entries, quizzes, contests and more!

❧

Contents

	Acknowledgments	vii
	Prologue	ix
Chapter 1	Fifty-five Percent	1
Chapter 2	Pack your PJs!	13
Chapter 3	Party Pooper	29
Chapter 4	The Class Project	39
Chapter 5	Travel to Tomorrow	47
Chapter 6	Wake up and Smell the Coffee	57
Chapter 7	Going, Going, Gone . . .	65
Chapter 8	No News is Bad News	75
Chapter 9	It Ain't Like it Used to Be	91
Chapter 10	Round the Bend and Outta the Park	103
Chapter 11	Fancy Meeting You Here	113
Chapter 12	What's Past is . . . Present	127
Chapter 13	Only You	141
Chapter 14	Duck and Cover	153
Chapter 15	Sincerely	165
Chapter 16	See You Later, Alligator	175
Chapter 17	A Stitch in Time	183
Chapter 18	Friday the 13th	195
Chapter 19	Doubleheader	205
Chapter 20	Rock Around the Clock	219
Chapter 21	Once in a Lifetime	231
Chapter 22	Glossary	235

Acknowledgments

Special acknowledgment goes to my editor and friend, Lori Van Houten, and my outstanding copy editor, Liz Butterfield. You're both a pleasure to work with and make my job so much easier! Phebe Telschow fed and nurtured us on more occasions than we can count (I owe you some fabulous shoes). A special thanks to Beth Groene for reading the manuscript and giving valuable feedback. I am indebted to Elliott Risch for explaining time travel theory to me and to adorable Jacqueline Meyncke for letting me borrow him. I'm honored to have the talented Astrid Sheckels providing the artwork for this book. My heart overflows with gratitude for my grandpa, Scott Wilson, and his ongoing support and encouragement.

Prologue

Dear Diary,   4th of May, 1955

Tomorrow the girls and I are doing our "Travel to Tomorrow"
project for Miss Boggs. Some of the gals (for instance, even
though I am not naming names –
Maxine) think it is a waste of time
(do you get the irony? Time?).
But I am personally thrilled. It'll be
a kick! I just know we'll have the
best project in class and then I'll have straight As! I finally
have it made in the shade. I'll tell you all about it tomorrow
night!

Always,
Mary Jane Donovan

PS- I'm wearing the plaid skirt I made in Home Ec.
PPS- Danny, Patty or Maggie: **Stop reading my diary!**

Dear Future Maxine,

I'm writing this letter to you from 1955. Remember the Travel to Tomorrow project that you did for Social Studies and got an A on? That is what I am doing today with those four chicks that you were never really tight with. When we started this project, "I had nothing to offer anybody except my own confusion" (Jack Kerouac). I am anxious to see what life really holds for us in 55 years. May there be peace on earth at long last. Remember, "feet, what do I need you for when I have wings to fly?" (Frida Kahlo).

With love and peace,
Yourself, Maxine

Dear Diary,   May 4, 1955

I am sad. Today we are doing our future project for Miss B. I worry that I will   not see these girls again. We have spent a lot of time together the last few weeks; I am also worried that I won't cast an eyeball at Beverly's brother Bob any more. When we studied at his house I saw him and he is dreamier than Cary Grant. I wonder if he noticed me? I don't know why he would. He's the most! He's tall, dark and handsome, and a big tickle! He reminds me of Desi (Lucy's Desi, not our cat Desi), even though Bob is, of course, not Cuban. But according to Maxine, it wouldn't matter if he was Cuban! Mom says Bob and Gary are practically twins. and she feels bad for Mrs. Jenkins. I've told Mom that they aren't twins and they're rich so she shouldn't feel bad. Mary's mom does have twins (and the Donovans aren't rich!). Anyway, Diary. Keep your fingers crossed. I am telling you my wish: marry Bob and move to Hollywood and be a movie star. Even when I am rich and famous, and have my pick of the boys, I would still choose dreamy Bob! Your Everlovin' (this is how John Wayne signs his letters),

Real Gone,   ~~Judy White~~ - Mrs. Robert Jenkins -

Mom,
Today I have softball. Bob and Gary will give me a ride after practice. I will help you make dinner when I get home since it is Mrs. Branislav's day to split.

Love,
Bev

P.S. Today is my future project at school. Wish me luck!

Dearest Irina,   4 May, 1955

Thank you for your last letter. I hope everything in Yugoslavia is good. Sorry it has taken me so long to write you back; I have been walking Alex to and from school, trying to improve my math grade, and working on a large flower painting. What's taken much of my time is a project for school called Travel to Tomorrow. I have to work with four other girls on what life will be like 55 years from now! One thing I know, we'd still be cousins and the best of friends. Will you live in America? Will I live in Yugoslavia? I hope we are together wherever we end up (I still hope New York City). I'll write more later and tell you how the project goes. And to answer your question: yes, I like a boy at my school. His name is James and he is very bright. I hope you two will meet someday . . . right after I meet him!

Ann

Dear Diary,   5th of May ????

I thought I was having a weird dream and that writing in my diary would help. But I'm still dreaming . . . I hope. Or this is some elaborate hoax. . . I woke up this morning and something felt strange. Everything is different--**EVERYTHING!!** Or else I'm different and everything else is the same. Everything is loud and bright and fast. . .my house is different, my family is different! I can't write any more. I need to do some research! I'm having a cow!

Always ?
Mary Jane

PS- I'm wearing the pink circle skirt I made in Home Ec.
PPS- Danny, Patty or Maggie: **Stop reading my diary!**

Dear Maxine,

In response to your letter to your future self . . . I think I'm the future self. I know it sounds crazy . . . but I think I woke up in the future this morning!! Or I've flipped. But I'm the same age, so how can it be the future?? The words of Jack Kerouac keep parading through my mind –

"Offer them what they secretly want and they of course immediately become panic-stricken."

Panic-stricken is an understatement.

–M.E.M.

Dear Diary,

I am scared! Something happened with our future project for Miss B. At least I think that was it. I woke up this morning in another world! I hope Bob is O.K. And I hope my new girlfriends are O.K.! And I hope Susan is O.K.! This would make a cool flick, but more of a horror movie than action. I'll keep you in orbit. Of course.

Judy.

Mom,

Where are you? Please come talk to me in my room as soon as you get home and get this note. I think I'm not feeling well. I actually feel fine, but everything is not fine. Please come find me when you get home.

Love,
Bev

Dearest Irina,   May?

I just wrote you yesterday and today I don't know where you are! I just looked on a map and there is no Yugoslavia! I don't know where you are and I don't know when I am. I am—

Desperate,

—Ann

1

Fifty-five Percent

Honey glazed sunshine streamed through the tall, paned windows. Students in the back row squinted their eyes in the warm light. One student averted her eyes by looking at the high ceiling to notice for the first time the water stains and crumbling plaster that accented most of the ceilings at Roosevelt High. The school building was an old red brick monstrosity; very different from the one-story rambling dust-colored schools that had been sprouting up like weeds in the new suburban neighborhoods all across the country after World War II.

Miss Boggs, the social studies teacher, wasn't distracted by things like glaring sunshine or stained plaster. She was all business, as always. Even though she was strict, the short, compact woman commanded affection from her students. An "A" was hard-earned in her class. She wasn't easily moved, except when making historical references. She would become so animated and talk in such detail, the students felt like it was almost as if Miss Boggs had actually *witnessed* the signing of the Declaration of Independence, the beheading of the Queen, or the burning at the stake of various martyrs.

Today Miss Boggs had that sparkle in her eye again as she announced the end of the term assignment that she hoped the students would be as excited about as she was. In only her second year of teaching, she aspired to make social studies interesting–no, more than that–*relevant* to her students, five in particular, and had received special permission from Principal Jones to alter her curriculum.

When introducing the class-wide assignment, she got the usual responses: heavy sighs, raised eyebrows, eager note-taking and no response at all from the daydreamers who were staring out the window and not listening.

"And I will put you into groups of five so that we have five groups total," Miss Boggs said, adjusting the aqua-colored cateye glasses on the end of her nose and looking at her notes. Her short, curled brunette hair was perfectly lacquered to her head and her fingernails gleamed long, oval and red. In a full gray skirt that fell mid-calf, she was as usual, simply-dressed. Everything about Miss May Boggs was modest, with one exception: the ornate gold wristwatch that she was never without, which glinted so merrily under the classroom lights that it attracted the attention of even the daydreamers.

Judy White, one of the daydreamers, was focused on Miss Boggs's fingernails, and how she had the lovely hands of a Hollywood starlet, when she suddenly heard her own name.

"Yes, ma'am," Judy answered, trying to appear awake and respectful.

"I was just reading your name off as part of your group," Miss Boggs said, knowing that she had caught Judy wandering.

Judy blushed. "Yes, ma'am," she repeated and slunk a little behind her small desk.

"Beverly Jenkins, Maxine Marshall, Mary Donovan, and Anna Branislav."

Ann, who had been gazing out the window studying the patterns the thin clouds made in the sky and what paint colors she would mix to capture the depth of blue, winced involuntarily upon hearing her given name. She preferred *Ann* to Anna; it sounded more American and less . . . well, *communist*.

"Miss Boggs?" Mary Donovan raised her hand. Maxine Marshall rolled her eyes. *Here goes Mary, the only girl in class who consistently called attention to herself deliberately by asking questions. What an actor!* Maxine's parents had raised her to not attract unnecessary attention to herself; she got enough attention just for being the only dark-skinned girl in most of her classes. Thank goodness her cousin Conrad was in this class or she'd be the only misfit.

"Yes, Mary?" Miss Boggs said, smiling as she turned back from the chalkboard where she was about to illustrate the points of the project in more detail. She already knew what Mary would ask.

"What percentage of our class grade will this project represent?" questioned Mary, her pencil at the ready to jot down the answer. Her shiny ginger-colored hair was pulled back into a perfectly tidy ponytail and nicely accented with a turquoise chiffon scarf used as a bow. Her cat-eye glasses, unlike Miss Boggs's, were resting in the just-right spot on the bridge of her nose. She smelled like Ivory soap. Everything about the redhead seemed squeaky clean, right down to her attitude in class. *I'll bet she made that skirt,* Maxine couldn't help thinking now with a spark of admiration, glancing at Mary's green and white plaid wool circle skirt that grazed Mary's freshly polished saddle shoes. Maxine could appreciate someone industrious and talented enough to make something on her own. And Mary was earthbound; that had to be a good sign for their project together, even if she was a bore.

Beverly Jenkins shifted uncomfortably in her seat. *Please God,* she prayed. *I don't ask for much—apart from whenever I ask you to help me win a game—but please let this be just a tiny percentage of our—*

"Class, this project, called Travel to Tomorrow, will be fifty-five percent of each of your social studies semester grades," Miss Boggs declared, punctuating her statement by writing it on the blackboard vigorously. Her nails dragged against the surface, making a terribly ominous noise and the class cringed, not only at the unbearable sound, but at the injustice of the percentage. She seemed not to hear it as she continued with increasing enthusiasm, "As you recall, all semester we've been learning about current events in a historical context in which we can identify cycles and connections with our past. Therefore, a project in which you will envision the *future* will be based on what you know about historical events, current events, and where those events may lead. This is your opportunity to pour yourself into the future." Miss Boggs emphasized every word and seemed to be overcome with an excessive nervous energy the more she spoke.

Mary nodded wholeheartedly, her ponytail bobbing. She looked at the other girls in her group. None of them seemed nearly as intrigued by this project as she was. Beverly, with her sloppy pony tail and sneakers (*who wears tennis shoes to school, anyway? Physical education is only one class in the day*), was fidgeting with her pencil; Maxine looked intimidating with her dark exotic looks and rolled-up blue jeans; Judy in her stylish pink poodle skirt and cute blonde hair beribboned in pig tails looked easily distractible; and Ann had the faintest accent and looked like she belonged on a gondola in Venice–*did she even speak English properly? Clearly*, Mary decided, *I will have to take charge on this one.* She thought of fifty-five percent of her grade relying on these four and sighed at her ragtag group. From the outside, a girl jock, a misfit, a goof, a Red, and herself—a square—didn't exactly look like the academic dream team.

They were going nowhere fast, even with Mary's clear, handwritten agenda and outline. But she wasn't getting any input from the others—or rather, the input she was getting wasn't real keen.

They were in the library after school, and each had somewhere else she'd rather be. Mary found herself saying "Fifty-five percent of our grades!" over and over like a broken record. She needed to call upon the patience she often exercised at home with her younger siblings, Danny, who was four and impossible, and twins Patty and Maggie, aged ten. Even though Nana had moved in to help Mary's mom, Mrs. Donovan, when Mary's father had left, those kids were still a handful and Mary knew it was her duty to help out. She had lots of practice at being patient and she could tell she was going to have more practice with the girls in her class project.

"While I can appreciate how handsome Humphrey Bogart was in *The Desperate Hours*," Mary said calmly to Judy about the movie she had just seen at the drive-in, "I must say that unless we get cranking on this project, we'll have our *own* desperate hours."

Judy looked scolded, but Beverly suppressed a snort of laughter.

"I think we should each take a section and present what is most meaningful to us," Ann spoke softly. "For example, I could take art, Beverly could take sports . . . ." She looked at Maxine, drew a blank, glanced at Judy. "Judy could take–"

"The movies! And the future of television! And Hollywood!" Judy said excitedly.

"Well, that's what I was trying to say we should do," Mary said, bluffing a little. It was actually a good idea, she wished she had come up with it. "Maxine, what would you like?"

"I don't know," Maxine looked thoughtful.

"Politics?" Ann offered.

Maxine seemed pleased. "I'll take politics," she agreed. "What about you?" Maxine asked Mary.

"Mary should have 'home life'!" Judy interjected, volunteering Mary for the last thing that Mary would have requested.

"Fine," she said quietly and flushed involuntarily. She resented how easily she blushed; with her red hair, fair skin and freckles, she seemed destined to spend most of her life looking like a splotchy pumpkin. She turned her attention to her notes and wrote,

Home life - Mary.

She thought of her father and made a heartfelt wish that in the future, parents could be more responsible and stay married for the good of their families. She would have to focus on that in the presentation. *Certainly, people would be smarter and even a little more kind in the future, wouldn't they?*

Beverly was reluctant to have the girls over to her house, even though it was the most logical place to meet (they were kicked out of the library for being too noisy, thanks for the most part to Judy's spontaneous squealing). Bev's reluctance stemmed from knowing that Ann's mother, Mrs. Branislav, would be on duty, working as Beverly's family's maid. *Would it be awkward for Ann?* Beverly wondered. Though Ann's mother had been helping at Beverly's house for as long as she could remember, Beverly rarely had contact with Ann other than classes at school. They just didn't run in the same circles. Well, that was just it, wasn't it? *Running.* Beverly was always running–in some sport or another. Her only friends were her teammates and only her teammates were her friends, with the exception of that bad news Diane Dunkelman who would always be her biggest competition, even when they were on the same team.

The girls had all readily agreed to meet at the Jenkins house, including Ann, who had showed no concern. Some agreed more readily than others, like Judy, who seemed especially enthusiastic to come to Beverly's house after school; that is, until Beverly mentioned it would be relatively quiet as her brothers would be at practice. Then Judy's excitement had dwindled quickly.

The girls arrived to the smell of the freshly baked cupcakes Mrs. Branislav had just set out.

"It smells divine!" Judy gushed, but then declined to have one as she insisted she must maintain a respectable weight if she were to succeed on television or in the movies.

They gathered around the kitchen table and Mrs. Branislav winked at her daughter, Ann, and then made herself scarce. Beverly's mother, on the other hand, swept into the room with freshly applied lipstick and a crisp clean apron that didn't seem to have seen much action other than the hot side of an iron. She crooned hello to everyone.

"It's so nice to have a house filled with girls for a change!" Mrs. Jenkins smiled. Beverly covered up her annoyance; her mother made it sound like Beverly had no friends. What she meant, of course, was that her sons filled the house with their maleness; everything revolved around them—the food, the laundering of all the jerseys and uniforms, the endless cleaning up after them. It was a whirlwind of *boy* at the Jenkins household. Even Mr. Jenkins's evening pipe left its scent behind, no matter how hard or long his wife or Mrs. Branislav cleaned during the day.

No guests at the Jenkins home would ever see a speck of dust or a stick of furniture out of place. The traditional dark walnut furniture was shined to a highly polished gloss, and the dainty davenport sofa and matching wing chairs had a lovely formal green, blue and rose colored floral pattern that coordinated perfectly with the curtains of the same fabric which were cleaned four times a year at exactly the same time, the first day of each season. No one in the family was allowed to actually sit on that furniture; it was reserved for company. The oversized matching brass lamps placed strategically around the room provided just the right homey glow. With five kids, four of them boys (and one grown-up boy in Mr. Jenkins), Mrs. Jenkins–with the help of Mrs. B–had to run a tight ship.

Mary spoke up, ever the polite one. "Mrs. Jenkins, thank you for having us to your lovely home."

"You're certainly welcome, dear. Just make yourselves at home and call me or Mrs. Branislav if you need a thing."

At the mention of Ann's mother, Beverly's eyes darted to Ann for a reaction. The others looked Ann's way, too, as Mrs. Jenkins excused herself.

"Looks like two of us have mothers here today," Ann said and gave Beverly a reassuring smile.

"Oh, your mother works here?" Maxine asked. Not many people had white maids. Maxine wondered how much money the Jenkins must have to hire a white maid instead of someone from her neighborhood. Maxine's mother and grandmother were maids, and her great-grandmother was a slave until she was Maxine's age. Maxine still had the quill her great-grandmother bought herself to celebrate her freedom. Some slaves could read, but writing was discouraged, since it was a symbol of status. It had taken generations, but Maxine and her sister were determined to break the cycle of servitude. Knowing now that Ann's mother was a maid, Maxine felt an immediate affinity with her new friend.

Ann offered Maxine a cupcake and nodded in response to Maxine's question.

"She's like one of the family," Beverly remarked about Ann's mother, known as Mrs. B by the Jenkins. Maxine had heard those very words about her mother and grandmother.

"So that makes *you two* family," Judy mused, pointing at Beverly and Ann and keeping an envious eye on Maxine as Maxine unwrapped her cupcake.

"I guess it does," Ann said with a smile.

This was all fine and dandy, Mary thought, but they had a lot of work to do. "We should get going on our project," she said, opening her folder and adjusting her peepers. Those who weren't licking frosting or reaching for a cupcake followed Mary's lead and opened their folders, half expecting Mary's battle cry, "Fifty-five percent of our grades!"

Judy put her yellow number two pencil in her mouth and looked dreamily out the kitchen window. It was mid-spring and except for a few ailing daffodils and tulips, the other flowers hadn't blossomed yet. The window box outside Beverly's kitchen was bare.

"I wonder what it would be like to be a teenager in the future," Judy mused.

Ann looked thoughtful as she took a bite from her cupcake. She recognized the recipe with her first bite. One of her mother's many specialties was baked goods. It was probably even Kosher, not that the Jenkins family would have cared. But Ann's mother did care and often snuck her own family's *parve* recipes in the Jenkins' family menu. "That would sure be a more interesting way to do our project," Ann said.

"I dig it!" Bev said.

"I hate to be a party pooper," said Mary, "but I really don't think that's what Miss Boggs had in mind. It doesn't sound very academic."

Maxine asked, "But why not? Why don't we imagine what our lives will be like as teenagers in the future, not just what the world will be like; we'll still incorporate history and all that."

The other girls nodded enthusiastically and Mary was forced to agree. She had her doubts, though, that Miss Boggs would think they were taking the assignment seriously enough. She wanted nothing more than to impress Miss Boggs. Mary liked to think that all her teachers held a certain standard for Mary, especially Miss Boggs, and she felt a bond with her social studies teacher because of it. As Mary thought admiringly of Miss Boggs, the girls had moved on, now excited about the project.

" . . . and we can just stick with our topics," Beverly said, as Mary was hoping she could switch from "home life." But everyone once again nodded enthusiastically, leaving Mary in the minority of one.

Just then the kitchen door burst open. A gust of air surged indoors and dramatically swished the red and white gingham curtains that framed the window in the top half of the Dutch door.

"Mom!" bellowed a deep male voice.

"Hi, Bob!" Judy burst out before she could stop herself. It was then that the tall strapping sophomore noticed the girls at the table.

"Oh, hey," he said and gave his little sister Beverly's pony tail a tug.

Mrs. Jenkins came in the room, closing the door behind Bob. "Robert, *hay* is for horses," she said, taking his books and his lunch sack.

"Cool. Cupcakes!" he said, making a beeline for the girls' table.

"No!" Beverly protested. "*Mother!*"

"Oh, he can have mine," Judy offered, quickly swiping up a cupcake to offer it to him; only she was a little too quick and the cupcake dumped frosting-side-down right in Mary's lap.

"Oh, no!" Mary exclaimed, jumping up and throwing the cupcake on the table. Her cream-colored wool skirt would now have a grody chocolate stain on it.

As Judy was rushing to apologize and reach for a napkin, Bob was whisked out of the room by his mother, encouraged to take a shower for dinner. Judy had missed hanging with Bob in his own house.

What a disaster, thought Judy.

What a disaster, thought Mary.

What a disaster, thought Beverly.

Maxine looked at Mary's skirt and thought, *What a disaster*.

These are delicious cupcakes, as usual, thought Ann.

2

Pack your PJs!

Bev went to bed early to get up for her morning run. Before she could shut her thoughts off for the night for sleep to ease over her, she went over her day while she blinked sleepily at the pennants hanging neatly on the light green walls of her bedroom. There was the orange and white pennant of the Roosevelt Indians, her school mascot; one for the red and white St. Louis Cardinals; even an old one from the St. Louis Browns (who were the Baltimore Orioles as of last year, she had to keep reminding herself); and the newspaper clipping of Stan Musial's five home runs the year before in a double-header against the Giants.

She still felt a thrill thinking of that game: her Pops ended up taking her at the last minute when her oldest brother Larry fell ill. It was her first Cardinals game; all her brothers had been before with Pops. She found herself truly fascinated by the bright green of the field, the men in their crisp uniforms, all in their places and playing their parts with such ease and skill, and the excitement of the crowd. Even the smell of the ballpark—the grass, peanuts and sweat—was appealing. Pops kept saying to everyone around them, "She likes it, she really likes it!" with such pride in his voice that it made the day that much more perfect. From then on, she was a goner for sports, especially baseball and softball. She even had her own wooden Louisville Slugger that she batted with whenever she played with her brothers. In fact, even when she wasn't hitting hard balls with it, it was always within reach when she was doing homework or just hanging out in her room. Along with her All-American Girls Professional Baseball League pennant, it was her most prized possession.

The girls' league had folded last year, but Beverly was determined to revive it somehow or otherwise find a way to play sports for a living. Her brother Larry had gotten an athletic scholarship to college and had played football before he was injured; she wondered why she shouldn't be able to get an athletic scholarship, too. She could knock a ball out of the park just as well as any of her brothers, and certainly better than Gary, who was more interested piano scales than batting averages.

With a strange tingling sensation, like the feeling in your bones before a big storm, her thoughts were a cyclone of baseball, the girls' league, a boy she'd been watching at school (and knew she shouldn't be thinking about), and the girls with whom she was doing the Travel to Tomorrow project. Finally, she reached for her bat and put it next to her in bed. Having her Louisville Slugger so close helped her fall asleep almost instantly.

Ann sat on her bed, caressing the fine bristles of the large, round, red sable paintbrush that had once belonged to her grandmother. When her parents left Belgrade, Yugoslavia, it was one of the few possessions besides clothing that they took with them. Ann's grandparents on both sides were Zionists, working toward establishing a homeland for Jews. Her grandparents had seen a nice fit between Ann's parents, Katrina and Ivan, politically, religiously and socially. But none of them had counted on the independent streak Katrina and Ivan had in common. They were not interested in being revolutionaries, nor in finding a homeland for their people; they just wanted to be left alone to work with their hands and raise a family. Their families accused them of being naive and even self-serving, but that didn't stop Katrina and Ivan from dreaming of America. They had set their sights on the United States even before Hitler advanced into Yugoslavia, tearing it apart and driving many Jews to financial ruin before killing them outright or starving them in camps.

When Ivan and Katrina left for America in 1937, their families regretted arranging their marriage and felt betrayed by the newlyweds' abandonment of their country. Only Katrina's mother, Ann's Bubbe, Nika, secretly gave them her blessing, passing on to them several pieces of the family's silver along with her favorite paintbrush that she had brought to Yugoslavia as a young Russian bride. Three years later, Ann was born as an American citizen. But Ivan and Katrina's joy at her arrival was overshadowed by the death of both of their parents; both of Ivan's brothers, Akim and Alexei; and Katrina's sister-in-law,

Zaria, at the Nazis' hands. Between both of their families, only Katrina's brother, David, and his toddler daughter, Irina, were among the very few surviving Jews in the whole country. Ann's mother, Katrina, had begged David to bring young Irina and join the Branislavs in the States, but David refused; his stubbornness to stay matched only by the determination of the Branislavs to leave.

Ann had never met her cousin Irina in person, but they wrote each other almost every day; more than pen pals, they considered themselves long-lost sisters. Ann couldn't imagine what Irina's life must be like in bleak Yugoslavia and longed for when Irina would be old enough to leave and they could get an apartment together in New York City.

In Ann's house, there was a blanket of unspoken sadness that was a permanent, invisible fixture. The Branislavs' observance of Kosher laws went even beyond an obedience to the Torah; it was a solemn tie to the family they would never see again.

Despite the sorrow that Ann's Bubbe's paintbrush should reasonably symbolize, Ann always felt inspired—delighted, even—when holding the brush. She knew it was her connection to her family in a happier way. She would rather think of the beautiful landscapes and beloved family faces her grandmother must have depicted with this brush than the devastation that was her end.

And now, as Ann felt the silken springiness of the sable bristles against the tips of her fingers, she had an idea for the Travel to Tomorrow project: she'd paint a portrait of herself in fifty-five years! She smiled to herself, certain this would have pleased her Bubbe Nika.

Sometimes Maxine's mama brought leftovers from her employer's dinner for Maxine's and her daddy's supper, and sometimes her mama made them their own dinner. But in either case, supper was invariably late in the evening due to the long hours both of her parents worked.

Tonight, as she flipped through the pages of her journal, her tummy was full from a spicy Cajun specialty of her mother's. In the other room, she heard her parents listening to a jazz record. Maxine felt like a traitor and wished she liked jazz as much as the rest of her family, but she couldn't help it: she preferred rock n' roll, even if her daddy did call it raucous loud white music. *That's OK*, Maxine thought. *White parents don't dig it either!*

She'd finished her homework, rolled her hair for tomorrow, and wasn't in the mood to read. She felt unsettled; in fact, she had felt this way since the class project had been assigned. Something about thinking too far into the future made her feel uneasy, wondering if the slow steps of progress the civil rights movement was making would be a bust or a boon. She eyed her great-grandmother's quill, which she kept on her nightstand (it had made its way from a place of honor in the living room to her room when her sister Melba left; maybe her parents hadn't mentioned it because they knew that it was a source of comfort for her). Colored men got a vote in her great-grandmother's lifetime, but not women. Now colored men and all women could vote, supposedly guaranteed by the 14th, 15th and 19th Amendments to the Constitution; but Maxine knew that it was still only on paper and many in her church had been discouraged, sometimes even violently, from voting. Her family lived in a small suburb that straddled the white and black halves of town; she lived in a sliver of limbo, and went to the only integrated school in the city. Even that integrated school was an accident, and not a result of last year's *Brown v. Board of Education* ruling that had outlawed segregated schools for black and white students, calling the "separate but equal" doctrine inherently *un*equal.

Maxine's mama, Gloria, worked as a housekeeper on a far side of town in a rich white neighborhood for a family Maxine had never met called the Johnsons, while her daddy worked for Stitson Heating and Cooling as a repairman. Every day he wore a blue crisp jumpsuit with "John" embroidered on a patch on the chest. Maxine couldn't stand how Mr. Stitson, the owner of Stitson Heating and Cooling, always referred to her Dad as "boy" instead of by the name stitched in bold black thread just below his left shoulder.

She had grown up observing how her parents were often treated as second-class citizens and how she walked a tightrope between two worlds: black and white. For generations, her family had seen laws come on to the books that rarely translated into everyday life. So what was that ever-present, nagging little tickle in her heart, especially when she held her great-grandmother's quill and thought with fondness of her sister Melba in college? She heard her mama singing in the other room and realized . . . it was *hope*.

Mary's mother, Jane Donovan, read a romance novel with a cigarette in one hand, and Nana had her embroidery in her lap—the television providing background noise for the two of them—while Mary sat on the floor leaning up against the sofa near Nana's slippered feet. Mary's sisters, twins Patty and Maggie, with little brother Danny between them, lay on their stomachs staring up at the TV trying to figure out what the "secret" was before the rest of the audience on *I've Got a Secret*. They liked the show well enough, but were biding their time until *I Love Lucy*, which was coming on next.

Mary, who was usually the most vocal guesser in the family, was preoccupied and fidgety tonight. She couldn't stop thinking about the Travel to Tomorrow project and how it was fifty-five percent of her grade. Normally, she had great respect and admiration for Miss Boggs, but with this project, Mary couldn't help questioning Miss Boggs's sense of justice. Why should more than half of Mary's semester grade have to rely so heavily on four other girls? They didn't even take it as seriously as Mary did. Plus, they had cornered her into a topic that she wasn't comfortable with. She preferred to depend on herself. The group thing cramped her style.

Finally, Mary excused herself to her room to work more on the project. Except that she was distracted by her prized possession: her black shiny Singer Featherweight sewing machine. Nana had won it in a radio contest before they were even selling them in stores and gave it straight to Mary for an early birthday present. Mary kept it next to her bed in its matching black carrier at night, and brought it out to look at or use during the day. It took a great deal of concentration for her to do her homework when she really wanted to be sewing on her new machine. She'd made aprons for her mother and Nana; dishtowels, curtains and matching oven mitts; more circle skirts for herself than she could count; and even matching frocks for Maggie and Patty. She had a spring dress pattern sitting on her desk waiting as her next project, right on top of a neatly folded stack of the most divine blue cotton.

It was silly, but that Singer was almost like a pet to her, a living, breathing companion with whom she could communicate. She sat on her bed now, running her hand across the top of the case and thinking about the class project. *Maybe,* she thought, *I'm going about this all wrong. Maybe instead of fighting the group project concept, I should go with it. Maybe I need to be more of a leader. Yes, that's it,* she decided. *Miss Boggs put me in this group for me to help them.* She gave a little pat to her sewing machine and then skipped back downstairs to get on the horn.

Elizabeth "Bitsy" White patted her curly blonde hair with one hand, and stroked the misty gray Persian cat, Desi, with the other. She was nestled on the couch with Judy, whose hair, the same color as her mother's, was in rollers. They had just watched the evening news after enjoying TV dinners and now they waited for Judy's favorite show to come on.

As was her tradition, Judy had her small white leather autograph book trimmed in gold sitting next to her. It was her most valuable possession. On the first page was her daddy's signature with a funny little sketch of a flower with a face. He'd signed it before he was shipped out to Korea. Then a couple of summers ago, Bitsy White had taken her daughter to Hollywood for a girls' trip and they went to all the TV and movie studios; when people found out that her father had been killed while serving his country, doors opened for them and they were treated like royalty. Judy had gotten autographs from Lucille Ball and Desi Arnaz, Jack Webb, Natalie Wood, Jack Benny, Gene Autry, Montgomery Clift, and even Marilyn Monroe, among others. Her mom had been promising her a return trip just so she could get James Dean's autograph, too.

The news had just updated them on the first couple, President Ike and First Lady Mamie Eisenhower. Everyone loved the President and his wife, but no one more than Judy's mom. Bitsy would remind her daughter over and over that even though President Eisenhower was a war hero himself, he did his best to not prolong the Korean War, a point that to Bitsy, herself a war widow, was very important. Though the President's actions came too late to spare her husband's life, still she couldn't help but admire the Commander-in-Chief.

And ever since Bitsy had gotten hold of Mamie's Million Dollar Fudge recipe in *Life* magazine, she was equally enthralled with the First Lady. The fudge was cheap and easy to make–even for someone who wasn't very proficient in the kitchen–and garnered Bitsy lots of praise, which she didn't often get for her cooking. She probably got the same comments, she liked to surmise, that Mrs. Eisenhower herself received when she served the fudge at the White House.

"Rock Hudson is going to be on *I Love Lucy* tonight," Judy said for the 800th time. She was in her pink and blue striped pajamas, even though it wasn't time for bed. Her mom was in her pink satin bathrobe and was now brushing cat hair off of it.

Lucy was Judy's favorite show and arguably her current most favorite actress. Although lately she also idolized Doris Day, since Judy thought her own mother looked a little like her. Plus she loved Doris Day and James Cagney in *Love Me or Leave Me*. But the real reason watching *I Love Lucy* was special was because it was her time with her mom that no one else could interrupt. . . .

The phone rang and Desi hopped off Bitsy with a start, then stalked across the room in a kitty huff.

"Mom, it's nearly on!" said Judy.

"I know, sugar. I'll make it quick." Her mom flounced out of the living room to the kitchen, with her robe flowing behind her like shimmering pink water. Judy thought admiringly how glamorous her mother looked tonight, even though every evening when she got home from work, she seemed exhausted.

After answering the phone, Bitsy returned quickly, with a freshly lit cigarette that made her look even more like a Hollywood starlet. "It's for you, Jujube," she said. "It's your friend Mary from school." She blew the smoke out in a thin line that curled upward.

Judy sighed. *Mary was not going to give up on this school project until she drove everyone ape!* Judy had had a spark of hope when the phone rang that it might be her best friend, Susan, who had moved away with her family after Christmas. Susan and Judy had met on the base from which Judy's dad was deployed for his last mission and had been friends ever since, calling and writing and visiting whenever they could. Judy was looking forward to summer vacation beginning in a month, when Susan planned to visit for a week.

With dramatic effort, Judy untangled herself from the Afghan blanket on her lap and moved with great speed to the kitchen phone, keeping one eye on the television set.

"Hello?"

"Judy, hi, it's Mary Jane Donovan from school?" Time was ticking; must she use her *middle* name?

Judy tried to remain polite. "Hi, Mary."

"I know I'm calling at a bad time, I know *Lucy*'s starting any minute."

Well, that helped endear her to Judy. "Rock Hudson's going to be on," Judy pointed out.

"Yes, I know. I'm going to watch it, too. Look, I'm a little concerned about our school project . . . " Mary seemed nervous. She almost added, "and it's fifty-five percent of our grade!" but stopped herself.

Judy waited.

"Maybe there's a time this weekend we could get together?" Mary asserted.

"Cool," Judy said, trying to hurry things along, wrapping the phone cord around her finger. Her mother hated it when she did that; the cord got all kinky and tangled.

"Maybe . . . we could have a sleep-over?"

Judy didn't wait to be prompted further as the theme music to her show swelled in the other room. "Why don't we have it at my pad?" she said, only half-realizing what she had just proposed.

"Really? Oh Judy, that would be the most! I'll call the girls. Friday night, then?"

"Swell," Judy agreed. At the first commercial, she asked her mom, who said yes. Her mom said yes to most things; Judy didn't even have a bed time and could stay up watching TV all night if she wanted to . . . if the stations didn't go off the air at midnight.

Judy had a little thrill of hope. Maybe a slumber party would help her feel better about missing Susan. And it could be a blast.

The doorbell rang. Judy wasn't ready! Her hair was still in a scarf and she had been cleaning and scrubbing the moment she'd scrambled home after school on Friday. She'd left herself a half hour for her beauty routine before the girls were expected. She shoved the Hoover into the closet near the kitchen and grabbed the scarf off her head as she hurried to the door.

Mary was on the front doorstep in a lightweight overcoat, matching hat, white-gloved hands grasping a sleeping bag, overnight case and Christmas tin balancing on top of it all. "Hi!" she said brightly. She nodded to the car in the street and her mother pulled away with a wave and a smile. "I came early to see if I could help you get ready."

"Come in," Judy said hospitably. It was hard to be angry at Mary for coming early when she looked so eager. "Did you bring the kitchen sink, too?" Judy joked, giving Mary a hand with her things.

Mary blushed a little. "Well, I have my school things, my pajamas . . ."

"I'm only teasing," Judy said cheerfully, leading Mary into the living room. "Mom's not home from work yet, but she said we could sleep in the living room. My room's not really big enough.

But look, we have sounds in here!" She pointed to the record player next to the TV as she put Mary's sleeping bag next to the sofa.

Mary placed her overnight case next to the sleeping bag and took in her surroundings. She couldn't help think of her ruined wool skirt when she noticed the sleek cream-colored sofa. She thought, *I guess Judy doesn't eat cupcakes in the living room*, and then berated herself for being impolite to her hostess, even silently.

Still, it was obvious the home was not exactly designed with children or family in mind. Everything was sleek and clean and trendy. The living room, smelling faintly of cigarettes just like Mary's house, had a slightly vaulted ceiling with white beams. A wide modern brick fireplace in the far corner was also painted white and the walls were a lemon yellow. At the front of the house, near the front door, two floor-to-ceiling windows were obscured by long white drapes. A pair of turquoise plastic chairs flanked the large 21" TV set and record player next to it, which the sofa faced. Mary's home couldn't have been more different: an old two-story Victorian filled with mismatched antiques and knickknacks, every surface draped with one of Nana's hand-crocheted doilies.

"We have a color TV," Judy volunteered. She didn't want to brag, but she was excited about their newest addition. The smaller, black and white TV now sat in the kitchen. Judy's mom had insisted that she would cook more if there was a TV in the kitchen, but so far it hadn't lessened the number of TV dinners Judy consumed. But Judy didn't mind. She didn't know of anyone else who had *two* television sets, not even the Jenkins.

"Gee, that's swell," Mary said. She started to take off her coat and remembered the round tin in her hand. "Oh, here's some fudge my Nana made for us," she said, offering the tin to Judy.

Judy laughed. "Mamie's Million Dollar Fudge?" Mary nodded and Judy told her that her mom had made a batch for the slumber party, too. They both chuckled and put the tin next to Judy's batch in the kitchen.

Mary asked how she could help, but since Judy was finished cleaning and vacuuming, the two went to Judy's room so Judy could freshen up. Mary involuntarily gasped as she passed through Judy's bedroom door. In sharp contrast to the clean mod sparseness of the rest of the house, Judy's room was papered floor to ceiling, wall to wall with photographs of movie stars—Cary Grant, Doris Day, Marilyn Monroe, Natalie Wood, and a special area devoted to James Dean.

Judy saw Mary eyeing the James Dean corner. "Isn't he the most? You know his mom died when he was nine and my father died when I was nine. Isn't that just weirdsville?"

Mary nodded, not realizing that Judy had lost her father. She wasn't a big fan of the *Rebel Without a Cause* incarnate, James Dean, but maybe that's because she was always hearing Nana complain about his "acute and chronic lack of morals."

Judy continued, "My dad died in Korea. Did yours die in Korea, too?"

Unprepared, and in classic Mary-style, she blushed and then fumbled with her words, "No, Dad's not . . . Well, he just doesn't live with us anymore." How had Judy known that Mary's father had cut out? One of the many reasons she didn't offer her house for the girls to study together in was because she didn't want to address the subject of her absent father. Fortunately,

Judy sensed correctly that this was not a topic for discussion, so she just said "oh" and went to her vanity, a white crescent-shaped desk trimmed in gold, which matched Judy's bureau, headboard and nightstand.

Judy gazed momentarily at herself in the three-way mirror and then glanced at the pictures embellishing the edges of its frame. Darn her freckles anyway; Doris Day didn't have freckles. Or if she did, she hid them well. She wished her mom would let her wear pancake makeup, but she told her daughter no, in no uncertain terms, because she would look like a "trollop." When she turned eighteen, Bitsy promised, Judy could wear all the makeup she wanted. Which was a good thing, because by then, she would hopefully be in the movies! She was also going to get her ears pierced.

"Do you ever wish you could get rid of your freckles?" Judy said, looking at Mary in the mirror, before she could realize the rudeness of her question. "Oh, I mean, you look beautiful–"

"Oh, all the time," said Mary, pushing up her glasses on her nose and sitting on the bed directly behind Judy. "I've done some research. Lemon juice makes them fade."

"Really?" Judy said excitedly. "I put lemon juice on my hair in the summer and it makes it blonder. I should try it on my face. Do you want to try with me some time?"

"Sure," said Mary, happy to have something to bond with Judy over.

Judy smiled happily and began brushing out her hair. "I'd like to be a cheerleader. Wouldn't that be the most?"

"You'd be a wonderful cheerleader," said Mary, doing a little cheerleading herself. Following Judy's lead, she tried straightening her pony tail, which had gone flat under the little hat she wore that was now on the glamorous white sofa in the living room. "Your hair is so pretty," Mary said. "I wish I had blonde hair," she confided, watching Judy gather her pale yellow curls into two pony tails.

"Oh, don't say that! You have red hair like Lucy! It's so unique, and–" she searched for the word and came up with "*exotic.*"

"Golly, I don't know about that," said Mary, but she was smiling.

3

Party Pooper

Maxine, Beverly and Ann crowded the small gray concrete front step of Judy's brick ranch house, ringing the bell and knocking repeatedly for fun. Mary followed Judy to the door and was relieved to see the other girls also looked like pack mules setting out on a long journey and didn't feel so bad for her load. Beverly managed a wave to her Pops, who had dropped them off in his pale green Buick, and the three squeezed through the door, passing some things to Mary and Judy.

"Wow," said Ann, looking around the vogue living room. "Fat city."

Judy hurried to set down the girls' things near the sofa and retrieved a magazine on the low-lying metal and maple coffee table. "See? We decorated it just like a starlet's house in Hollywood." She flipped the glossy *Architectural Digest* open to a page that did indeed echo the colors and feel of the room they all stood in. The big difference was the room in the magazine was much bigger and featured a wall of glass that overlooked a lush valley and part of the Hollywood sign (which was missing the last "O" and the top part of the first "O" so the sign really looked like "Hullywo d").

"It *feels* like we're in Hollywood," enthused Mary and this seemed to please Judy very much.

Judy had also brought out to the living room and strategically placed her autograph book, which she now showed them with pride, starting with her daddy's autograph.

"What's that one say?"

"Natalie Wood."

"Wow," Ann was impressed. She especially liked Natalie Wood, with whom she felt a special kinship because Natalie's parents had come from Russia, just as Ann's grandmother had.

With a happy glow after showing off her autograph book and her Hollywood-style home, Judy gathered coats and hats as Beverly passed Judy a bright blue tin. "This is from my mom—"

"Mamie's Million Dollar Fudge?" chorused Mary and Judy together.

"Yes. How did you . . . ?" Beverly watched as Mary and Judy broke out into giggles. Each girl, who had reservations about spending an entire night together, began to relax. Judy suggested they make a fire in the fireplace and make some popcorn before taking up their school project.

Judy started, "It is, after all—"

"—Fifty-five percent of our grades!" said Beverly, Maxine and Ann. Mary blushed, but they all laughed together.

Hours later, Mary in her plaid nightgown with giant ruffle around the collar, Beverly in one of her brother's old oversized T-shirts (*Bob's?* wondered Judy hopefully with a little pitter pat of her heart), and Judy in her striped satin PJs and bright green facial masque all sat on their respective sleeping bags between the sofa and the TV set. Ann and Maxine in their pajamas sat on the sofa, at least until it was time for bed and they'd join the others in the circle they made on the floor when they'd moved the coffee table out of the way. There were two giant bowls of popcorn between them and enough fudge to feed an army. There were five bottles of Coca-Cola, at various levels of emptiness.

The girls were starting to feel more and more comfortable with each other as the night progressed, which was good news since Ann was in rollers, Judy had her facial masque on, Maxine had a stuffed teddy bear and they were all in bedclothes. A warm blaze crackled in the fireplace behind Mary, causing the edges of her silhouette to glow in the firelight. Notebooks, pencils and paper were at the ready. But it was hard to focus on schoolwork on a Friday night at a slumber party. They had just danced themselves into a frenzy, playing "Rock Around the Clock" five times in a row on Judy's record player. Now they tried to catch their breath and focus.

"Beverly?" Judy asked, tossing one piece of popcorn in her mouth and trying to seem casual. "What's Bob up to tonight?"

"Bob?" Beverly asked. "My *brother*, Bob?"

Maxine giggled. She wore a scarf on her head to keep her dark curls smooth.

"Why are you laughing?" Judy said.

"It's obvious, isn't it?" Maxine said.

"Yes," piped up Ann.

"What's obvious?" Mary asked, concerned she had missed a vital piece of information.

"It doesn't take jets to see that you like Bob Jenkins!" Maxine said to Judy, playfully flinging popcorn at her.

"It's *obvious?*" Judy said, her eyes big.

Ann said, "To us it is."

"I didn't know that," Beverly said.

"I didn't either." Mary was worried that she hadn't picked up on that "obvious" detail; or else hadn't been told.

"Do you think Bob's hep to it?" asked Judy, half-eagerly, half-fearfully.

"Er . . . " Beverly considered carefully if Bob would know that Judy liked him. There were so many reasons he wouldn't know. Not the least of which was his unfortunate infatuation with that bad news Diane Dunkelman. "No, I don't think he knows."

"Well, don't tell him," Judy rushed to say. "Unless, of course, he *asks*." Judy had a glowy childlike expression which could be seen even through the green gook on her face. She was real gone, alright. "Say," Judy said, her expression changing slightly, "what do you think Miss Boggs's story is?"

"What do you mean?" Ann asked.

"Do you think she has a boyfriend?"

Mary found this line of questioning somehow inappropriate. You shouldn't know about your teachers' personal lives, should you?

"Well, how old do you think she is?" Bev wondered out loud.

"Oh, she's real old. Like twenty-five, maybe," Judy surmised.

"She must not have a boyfriend if she's giving us these big assignments that she has to grade on the weekends," Maxine reasoned. The others laughed. Mary didn't like this conversation at all. She felt a loyalty to Miss Boggs; she didn't want to gossip about her disrespectfully behind her back.

"I wonder if she's rich," Judy continued. "Have you seen that gold watch of hers? Maybe she's an heiress, or . . ."

In an effort to change the subject, Mary asked Judy about her facial mask. "Do you need to wash that stuff off?"

Judy brushed Mary's concern aside and found herself a new target. "What's *your* story, Mary? Who razzes your berries?" she asked Mary directly, hoping that Mary had a secret crush that she would divulge and spice up their party. Mary's plan to change the subject had succeeded, but this was not where she was hoping they would go . . .

"Uh . . . no one . . ." she stammered. She averted her eyes to her notebook, embarrassed. There was no one she particularly liked, unless you counted the love of her life, James O'Grady, the boy whose name filled her diary daily.

"I think Ann likes James O'Grady!" Maxine said mischievously, diverting attention from Mary.

Ann and Mary were equally shocked. All eyes went to Ann. Her mouth dropped open and she flung a pillow at Maxine. "How would you know that?"

Maxine smiled. "I saw you cast an eyeball on him in art class."

Dragnet, Judy's other cat, wandered in to make the scene. He snuck past Beverly to hop onto the sofa between Maxine and Ann, then went to join Desi near the hearth for a warm cat nap.

"He goes to my church," Mary said, maybe a little too loudly. "James does."

"Maybe you should start going to Mary's church," Maxine teased Ann.

"Oh, that would *kill* my parents," Ann laughed.

Curiosity piqued, and temporarily distracted from the subject of James O'Grady, Mary asked, "What do you mean?"

Ann said cautiously, "My family isn't . . . uh . . . Catholic."

Mary was on the verge of responding when Judy offered helpfully, "*I'm* not Catholic."

"Well, I wouldn't *think* so," sniffed Mary, feeling ruffled that Ann liked James, and feeling that familiar last-one-in-on-the-joke sensation which she so despised.

"Yeah, Judy's religion is Hollywood," Ann teased.

It took only the briefest of moments for Judy to decide this was an offensive remark and she retorted, "That's interesting coming from a *communist.*"

Like a plate shattering in a crowded restaurant, there was an immediate and stunned silence until Ann said quietly but firmly, "I am *not* a *communist.*"

It was one of the biggest insults of the day. All anyone had to do was call someone the "C" word and it was nearly as good as convicting them of a crime—the crime of being unpatriotic.

Mary was surprised that Judy would voice such a claim about Ann (secretly, she may have wondered herself, but would never be so crass as to utter it out loud). Certainly Judy was sensitive to the issue with so many of her beloved Hollywood stars being black-listed after having been falsely accused of being anti-American members of the Communist Party.

"Aren't you from the *Soviet Union?*" pressed Judy, oblivious to the tension in the air.

"My parents are from Yugoslavia," Ann said vehemently, clearly trying to remain calm. Her grandparents had been Communists, but that was because it was the lesser evil to Hitler's fascism. Her parents had come to the United States because they didn't want to be either one.

"Even if her parents *were* from the Soviet Union," spoke up Maxine tremulously, "that doesn't make *her* a Red!" It was easy for Maxine to speak up for her friend, but not so easy to speak up for herself after having been judged by the color of her skin her whole life.

Ann looked gratefully at Maxine, but the nearly tangible uneasiness in the room caused even the cats, who had been resting peacefully by the fire, to rouse themselves and exit the room without even stretching or passing by the girls for a pat. Judy's mom had retired to her room an hour before and was presumably sleeping by now.

"Where are *you* from?" Mary heard herself ask Maxine, and immediately regretted her own lack of discretion. Now all eyes were on Mary for speaking up and her stomach tightened. "I mean your neighborhood is . . . Why would you . . . ?" She faltered. She had been curious about Maxine's background and why Maxine and her cousin were going to her school instead of another school with more colored people. Mary didn't have a problem with it, she just was curious. She realized immediately that this was not the time or way to be asking.

"I'm from around the corner," said Maxine calmly, even as her fear of being singled out for her skin color was being realized. "I've *always* lived around the corner. And no, I'm *not* a communist, either."

Uncomfortable with any kind of confrontation that wasn't on a playing field, Beverly, who had managed to remain silent, was now frosted and burst out, "Why would you imply those terrible things about people you don't even know?" to Mary and Judy, whom she sat between on the floor. "You didn't like it when they accused Lucille Ball of being a communist. You couldn't have been keen on that," she said pointedly to Judy. "But they're . . ." she swallowed, "*we're* . . . your *friends.*"

A light switch appeared to have flipped on in Judy's mind. *Friends?* She hadn't dared to consider that they were becoming her friends. Suddenly, without warning, she burst into tears. This was almost as surprising as her accusation moments ago and the girls began to suppose that drama *would* be a good field for Judy to consider.

"Judy?" said Beverly, reaching toward her. She wasn't sure what to do. Maybe this was why she didn't have close friends. It wasn't as fun as people made it sound!

"Now look what you've done!" Mary said to Beverly.

Beverly was startled. "Me? You're the one who–"

"Don't jump on her!" sniffled Judy to Mary. She wouldn't have her future sister-in-law attacked by anyone.

Soon, everyone was screeching at everyone and no one in particular, until a high whistle cut through the chaos.

"Ladies!"

Bitsy, Judy's mom, stood near the hallway that led to her room. She wore her pink robe and her hair was neatly curled over big rollers.

The girls grew silent and sullen instantly.

"I've never heard such a racket, even at a slumber party. It doesn't sound like much fun."

"No, ma'am," murmured Judy. She lifted her head and with renewed energy, pointed her finger. "It's just that she–"

"Oh, no, you don't, Miss White. You are a better hostess than that. Treat your guests with respect. And all of you, if I have to come out again, I'll call your parents to come get you."

Mary's face burned red with shame and the other girls look fairly embarrassed, too. Maxine imagined how horrified her parents would be to have to come pick her up from a white family's house in the middle of the night because she wasn't behaving herself.

"Sorry, Mrs. White," they all muttered one after the other.

"You might try enjoying yourselves. That's what slumber parties are for," said Bitsy before uttering her final good night.

Maxine's teddy bear had fallen next to Beverly and she picked it up as a gesture of peace and because she wasn't sure what else to do.

"I'm sorry," wheezed Judy, sniffling now, totally embarrassed that her mom had stepped in. Her facial mask now had deep furrows carved from her tears.

"I'm sorry, too," said Mary softly.

It was no use getting any work done now, they were feeling drained and annoyed. Beverly clutched the teddy bear and added her apology.

I know one thing for certain about the future, thought Mary before falling into an exhausted sleep, *I won't be friends with these girls!*

Little did she know, there were four other girls tucked into their sleeping bags nursing the same certainty.

4

The Class Project

"This is a waste of our time," Maxine said out of the blue.

It was their last meeting, the evening before the presentation. Beverly couldn't have agreed more. She could be out running laps, training to outrun Diane Dunkelman instead of doing busywork. What a drag. But they were nearly finished anyway and she could go back to her athletics soon enough. Although she had to admit that getting together with this group was a nice break from being crowded by her brothers all the time.

"Why would you say that?" Mary said, taking Maxine's comment personally.

"Do we really think the world is going to change for the better in fifty-five years? Or that we could possibly know what it will be like?" Maxine sighed.

"It *has* to be better," Ann said fervently.

"Can we go over the order again?" Judy asked with a worried expression. She'd never seemed to care much about her grades before, but this was different. This amounted to a performance!

"Alright. But write it down if you have to!" Mary said. "First, we start with Maxine: world events and politics."

"I'm talking about how the world will be color-blind and we'll see the law and human rights as universal, not just applying to one particular race; I'll be able to go to whatever school or college I want to, ride the bus, go all the same places as white people." As Maxine spoke, trying to convince herself this would be the case, Judy thought of the incident a few days before, after the slumber party. They'd met at the five-and-dime drugstore to get chocolate malts and sodas and work on their project. Judy had noticed that they were getting some gawks from other store patrons because of Maxine's dark skin. Maxine, pretending to be unaware of the glances, had said to Judy, "Wouldn't it be funny if we judged people by the color of their eyes?"

Judy had really liked that comment and hoped Maxine could say something like that for the Travel to Tomorrow project. Now, in Judy's kitchen with the sun setting and making the white curtains glow pinky-orange, Maxine continued describing her section of the assignment: "When I turn eighteen, I will have a vote and when I get a job, I will have equal pay."

Maxine thought admiringly of her big sister, Melba, one of the first of her color and certainly the first woman in her family to go to a four-year university. Their parents worried for her safety, but Melba heroically insisted it be done for the sake of her children and her children's children. Maxine, who was usually an optimist, now hoped weakly that her sister's sacrifice wouldn't be in vain and prayed for her safety every night.

"Then it's Ann's turn," Mary said, without referring to her notes. She'd gone over it a million times and could do practically the whole presentation in her sleep, with the very big exception of her own section. She still resented having "home life" as her topic.

Ann adjusted the pretty lavender and yellow scarf around her neck. "I'm going to talk about how books won't be burned or banned anymore and art will be a regular part of education and a big part of everyone's lives. I'm working on a portrait of what I'll look like in fifty-five years." She shyly pulled a small sketch she'd been working on to translate to a larger canvas for her self-portrait in oil. It was a bold watercolor with an expressionistic and Cubism feel. But Ann knew she had a long way to go before completing it on canvas in time for the presentation of their project.

"Ooooh," breathed Judy. "I like it! Did *you* paint that?"

Ann nodded, pleased. "I just think of how Impressionism changed art forever; imagine what color will be in the future! I think that modern art will be more abstract and less representational." They all nodded in agreement, impressed with Ann's talent.

"Judy goes after Ann," Mary prodded.

Judy unconsciously touched her hair, making sure it was all in place and held up a small note before clearing her voice. "In the new century, we will see film and television going beyond entertainment and being a force for education," she said, projecting clearly. Mary was surprised at Judy's insight. She might actually have something there. "Hollywood stars will be pillars in the international community, leaders, because they share their artistic talent to help improve the world." Then all at once her authoritative demeanor shifted and she giggled. "Do you like it?"

They all nodded enthusiastically and after Judy finished her speech, Beverly was up next. "Year after year, mankind—"

"And womankind!" interjected Maxine.

"Of course," Beverly said, flustered, scratching a note on her paper. "Year after year, mankind *and womankind has,* er, *have* been excelling and progressing in athletics. Records are broken every year as people exceed seemingly impossible physical limits. Women will excel in professional leagues just as men do, and girls will have opportunities in school to exercise their athletic abilities."

"That's great, Bev," Mary said. "Just remember to speak up so we can hear you."

"Righto," said Maxine. "And now it's you," she said to Mary.

"Home life," Mary said. Then she drew a blank.

"You can use your notes," Ann encouraged.

Slowly, Mary held up a sheet of paper. It was blank.

"What have you been working on all this time?" Maxine asked, stunned, as the other girls gasped in surprise. Mary had been their fearless leader, but now had nothing to show of her own.

Mary was turning shades of scarlet that did not complement the light blue sweater set she wore. "I don't–" she stammered. "I don't like my topic."

"Why not?" asked Beverly.

Mary swallowed hard. She had to get it out, tell someone. Now she didn't much have a choice.

"My parents . . . are . . . *divorced.*" She whispered the bad word, ashamed.

The girls were silent.

"I just don't know what home life will be like in the future. I don't understand it now. I just hope it gets *better*," sniffled Mary.

"Just write down what you think. Remember we're looking at history and the trends that come out of it," Maxine said, knowing that she should be offering something much more helpful–and personal–than that.

"That's what I'm afraid of," said Mary. She had hoped to one day get married, but who was to say that her husband wouldn't grow tired of her or change his mind about his children and move on to something–some*one*–else? Mary couldn't imagine what would be worse. Unless it was being one of the children left behind . . .

"Maybe if it isn't so personal. You know, like Maxine said. Look at the trends." Judy surprised them all with her thoughtfulness. "There used to be arranged marriages, but it's outdated now–"

Ann averted her eyes. Her parents' marriage had been arranged when her parents were teenagers in Belgrade. Perhaps this wasn't the time to bring that up.

"So we can expect a change in the divorce rate, too," Beverly finished. "Maybe when people marry for love, they stay together for love. You'll find your dream man and have a house-load of ankle-biters!" It was easy to picture Mary with a multitude of kids. She was already such a mom. In thinking about love and marriage, Beverly's thought automatically wandered to her desperate hope that someday she herself could fall in love with whomever she wanted, regardless of what others thought about it.

"I guess so," Mary said, brightening slightly.

"And look at the world scene in fifty-five years," Maxine said, brightening up herself a bit. "If the world finally finds peace, then won't we find peace at home, too?"

"No more war," Judy said dreamily, imagining her own father at home with her and her mother.

"I'll bet life for a homemaker will be so much easier with advanced technology! Women can do something other than housekeeping. You can mention how robots will probably do most of the cleaning," Beverly suggested to Mary.

"So my mom will be replaced at your house by a robot?" Ann joked with Beverly.

"Your mom will have her *own* robot!" Beverly said cheerfully. Ann dug that idea. Since the world war had ended nearly ten years ago, she had hoped her parents wouldn't have to work as hard, but that hadn't been the case. She liked picturing her mom with her feet kicked up and some one–or something!–waiting on her for a change. Maxine imagined the same thing for her mother. What would her mother do with all that time? Could she have a career of her own?

Judy added, "And there won't be as much cooking because we'll probably have whole meals in a little pill!"

"Everything will be simpler." Maxine's deep brown eyes had regained their usual sparkle. She had her chin resting on her hand and for once allowed herself to be content to imagine what was to come.

"I can't wait for the future," Ann said wistfully.

"Me either," said Beverly and the other girls chimed in, agreeing.

"The future *will* be a simpler time—for *all* of us," Mary said, now convinced.

"OK, so the only thing left is to '*travel to tomorrow*'! Good luck, everybody!" Judy gave a cheerleader-type flourish and they all clapped.

She couldn't wait to tell Susan about her performance.

Beverly couldn't wait to get back to running.

Mary couldn't wait to have a close-knit family of her own.

Maxine couldn't wait until everyone of every color was free.

Ann couldn't wait to send her painting to her cousin, Irina.

Desi and Dragnet couldn't wait to be fed as they circled their empty food bowls near the back door, meowing at the obviously distracted five young ladies.

5

Travel to Tomorrow

Mary had met the girls after school at the five-and-dime for a goodbye (and good riddance!) malt. The other girls were giddy, but Mary was depressed by her presentation and had just wanted the day to be over already. It had not gone the way Mary had envisioned at all. They had blazed through their presentations too fast and Mary had stumbled through her section clumsily, refusing to look down at her notes, muttering and blushing her way through it.

While Mary slurped down the rest of her chocolate malt, Miss Boggs of all people came in to the five-and-dime. Usually, Mary would take this opportunity to say a bright hello to her favorite teacher. But this time she hung her head. It was Judy that called out, "Miss Boggs!" and waved her over.

Miss Boggs was pleased to find them all together. She crossed the black and white checkered floor, passed the ice cream counter and came to the round marble table where they were huddled together over their celebratory (or in Mary's case, consolatory) treats.

"How do you think we did?" Judy asked eagerly and, if anyone had bothered to ask Mary, without tact.

"Well, I still have to read your papers tonight," Miss Boggs answered diplomatically. Judy, Ann and Bev grinned, but Mary could tell by Miss Boggs's noncommittal response that so far, fifty-five percent of their grades was not looking swell.

"It was a hard assignment. We're just glad it's over," Maxine blurted out.

"Maxine!" Ann scolded and swatted Maxine's shoulder.

Miss Boggs gazed at all of them thoughtfully. Little did they know that they were the very reason she had dreamed up the assignment in the first place.

All of a sudden, she seemed much younger as her face took on a girlish glow. She leaned over their marble table, almost with a secretive air and took their hands. Her gold watch peeked out from under her glove and twinkled. A delicate perfume of lily of the valley wafted around them as she included herself in their circle. She took Mary's and Maxine's hands on either side of her, and the other girls all instinctively grabbed hands, holding their breath and gazing at her expectantly. The five-and-dime around them seemed to vanish.

Weirdsville, thought Ann and Beverly.

How odd, Mary thought.

I can't believe my teacher hangs out at the same five-and-dime as we do! marveled Judy.

Maxine glanced about to see who might be looking at her holding hands with a bunch of white girls, but there was no one around and the whole place seemed unnaturally still, as if the six of them were suspended in time.

"Promise me," Miss Boggs intoned quietly and forcefully, "that you will always be friends."

"OK," gulped Mary.

"I want to hear you say it . . . promise you'll be friends, even in fifty-five years!"

"We promise to be friends in fifty-five years," the girls all said together, wondering at the odd request of their normally reserved teacher.

Now Miss Boggs stood up straight and gave them a big warm smile. Maybe they hadn't missed the point of the assignment after all, she reassured herself.

"Enjoy your sodas, girls. I'll see you tomorrow in class with your graded papers."

As she left, she smoothed her curly hair with her white-gloved hand. Only Maxine noticed that Miss Boggs had come into the soda shop, talked to them, and left without getting anything for herself. It struck her as very peculiar.

But the other girls just sighed a breath of relief once their teacher was gone.

Judy and Ann giggled nervously.

"That Miss Boggs is an odd duck," Bev commented.

"Did we mean it?" Mary asked, staring out the door after Miss Boggs.

"Mean what?"

"That we'll be friends . . . even in fifty-five years?"

Maxine had planned on moving on with her life once this project was over. Bev was anticipating a life with far less female drama.

Judy said with all her heart, "Oh, yes!"

And spontaneously, the girls held hands once again, just briefly, to seal the pact.

Mary's alarm clanged an abnormal ruckus. She rolled over in bed, underneath the cozy hand-stitched patchwork quilt that Nana had made, and turned the offensive clock off. She usually woke up precisely one minute before her alarm so she could disengage it before it rang, but she felt exhausted this morning and slept right through her own mental wake up call.

She turned her head toward the window. Behind her gauzy pink curtains, she could see a clear day dawning. That was promising. Yesterday had been a bad day. She remembered the Travel to Tomorrow presentation with a groan and pulled the quilt over her head. In the darkness under the covers, she relived in horrifying detail her failed attempt at salvaging fifty-five percent of her grade. For some reason, when it had been her turn to talk, she could do nothing but turn red and stammer. She had refused to read from her notes. Judy had been outstanding, not looking at her notes once, and Mary had felt the pressure to try to be as fresh and spontaneous-sounding as Judy. She then thought of Miss Boggs's peculiar appearance at the five-and-dime after school . . . .

Mary was startled back to reality by a knock at her door as her little brother Danny raced by making as much noise as humanly possible on his way to breakfast.

Mary heard her mother call from downstairs. The day was in full swing and Mary felt like she was already behind. She slid out from under the quilt, running her hand across her sewing machine and tidying her bed. She glanced at herself in the mirror over her dresser. It would be hard to conceal her fatigue today. She deserved to wear her favorite skirt. Since her cream wool circle skirt bore the scar of chocolate, her new favorite skirt was a dreamy pale green. It brought out the color of her eyes. In case anybody (like James O'Grady) cared to notice.

Mary's mother called out for her again.

Mary swung her bedroom door open. "Coming, Mom!" She smelled coffee wafting up from the kitchen and was surprised by the amount of noise coming from downstairs. She shrugged and closed the door again to find her outfit and wait for her turn in the bathroom.

Her door burst open.

"Mom says *come on*," said Mary's little sister, Maggie.

"Please knock!" Mary squealed and then squinted at Maggie. "What are you wearing?"

"My SpongeBob t-shirt. Mom said I could. Hey!" she screamed at her twin, Patty, and left Mary standing befuddled in her room. She closed the door behind her little sister. *What in the heck is a spongebob?* wondered Mary as she cleaned off her glasses. She decided with the level of chaos in the house this morning to change in her room. She'd wash her face, put on powder and brush her teeth after breakfast.

She stacked her books neatly by her bedroom door and made her way to the kitchen for her morning meal.

At the bottom of the stairs, she felt like she had been hit by a tidal wave. Nana was sitting in the living room watching TV (*was that a color TV? We don't have a color TV!*), Mary's mom was in the kitchen holding a big mug of steaming coffee standing near the sink and talking into a small metal box. Maggie, Patty and Danny were chasing each other around the kitchen table.

"Give it back!" screeched Patty.

"Kids!" Jane Donovan hissed. "I'm on the phone!"

Mary then noticed with shock another color TV in the kitchen which was blaring in the corner. On it, a brightly dressed slick man and woman in a low-cut top argued loudly while words passed swiftly underneath them, above them and in black boxes on the side.

"I can't deal with this now," said Mrs. Donovan, slipping the small metal box into her pocket. She wore a blood-red suit, no panty hose and high heels. Her dark auburn hair was down, cut just below her ears and straight and silky. She wore big diamond earrings, the likes of which Mary had never seen, at least not in this part of town. Her mom muttered to herself, "What I wouldn't give for a cigarette . . . ."

"Mom?" Mary said incredulously. Had her mother stopped smoking? And why was she dressed in such a goofy getup with so much makeup on?

"Mary, your dad's coming to pick you and the kids up after school and taking you to dinner. I'm showing a house."

"You're . . . what?" Since when were her parents on speaking terms? Mary wondered as a strange buzzing filled her ears. And since when did her father come to see them?

"Kids! That is it! I have to leave. Now listen to your Nana. I can't handle this kind of stress; I need a staycation." Mary's mom alternated between mumbling and yelling. Mary stood frozen to her spot.

"Is that what you're wearing?" Mrs. Donovan looked her daughter up and down. "Is it history day at school? Do you want a breakfast bar? KIDS! For the love of Pete, will you sit down and finish your cereal?" Mrs. Donovan had taken the small metal box out of her pocket again, removed the sliding lid and was now fiddling with it.

"What is that?" Mary found her voice.

"Oh, I know. I said I hated texting, but I get so tired of talking on the phone. OK, sweetie. Have a good day. Mom," she called into the living room, "I'm taking off. Have fun working out! Kids, love you. Have a good day. Eat something!" And in one swift, heavily perfumed movement, she was out the back door.

Maggie and Patty chased Danny upstairs and Nana felt safe to come into the kitchen, past the spot where Mary was rooted to the ground.

"Do you want some cereal, honey?" Nana asked Mary, retrieving a bowl from above a shiny panel under the cabinets. Was that a *dishwasher*?

"Cereal . . . ? No, thanks," she said, wondering what had happened to their usual breakfast of sausage, eggs and oatmeal.

"Look at you," Nana said with a wink, pouring herself a bowl of thin brown flakes. "You know, you might be making fun, but there was a time I really dressed like that."

Mary looked down at her skirt, which somehow seemed very tame and out of place. What was going on? The buzzing in her ears was escalating to a roar. She wasn't feeling very well.

"Uh, Nana?" Mary stammered. "When? When did you dress like this?"

"In the 1950s, of course," said Nana, who was wearing thick cotton terry pants and a matching shirt. Mary had never seen her in pants.

"The 1950s," Mary repeated. "What . . . day is it today?"

"It's Thursday. Are you feeling alright?"

"But what month is it?" Mary's voice was now a hoarse whisper. She could not bring herself to ask what she really wanted to know.

"It's May. Mary, honey, do you need to stay home today?" She reached to touch Mary's forehead.

Mary pulled away. "Nana, do we have a newspaper?" Mary's knees were starting to buckle. This was weirdsville. What a dream! It all felt so real! She desperately wanted to wake up. If she didn't wake up soon, she might be late for school.

Nana was now holding her bowl of cereal soaking in milk staring at her granddaughter who looked to be getting paler by the moment. "You know we don't get the paper. We get all our news from cable and the Internet."

"From the . . . ?" Mary now had no choice. "Nana, what *year* is it?"

Nana laughed now, relieved that obviously Mary was joking around.

On her walk to school, Mary grew increasingly uneasy. When Nana had told her the year, Mary had nearly fainted. Now she watched as cars that looked like space ships rumbled past her with sounds like thunder pounding inside and kids called out the window, sometimes at her, sometimes just for the sheer noise of it. She clutched her books to her chest and kept her face averted. Her ponytail in its green scarf swung from side to side with each step. She was now determined to get to the bottom of this. *What would Nancy Drew do? She would gather clues, lay low, put it all together and solve the crime.* And that's what Mary would do.

In her first and second period classes, the kids and teachers were the same. Well, their names and faces were the same, but they were dressed funny, they slouched a lot and mostly the students didn't listen when the teacher was speaking. Some of the students even had little boxes like she saw her Mom with earlier. When the teacher saw one of them, he'd say, "No cell phones! You know the rules!" Besides the strange words people were using, she was feeling panicked about her home ec classroom: there were no sewing machines or kitchen equipment in it. They just sat in rows of desks and talked about budgets. She found herself desperate for fifth period to see the other girls and Miss Boggs and tell them about her perplexing experience.

And what was a sellfone, *anyway?* Mary wondered. She made a note to herself to find out. *Treat it like a clue,* she breathed, trying to remain calm. Maybe she should have had breakfast after all. But when she'd asked Nana for her usual sausage and eggs, Nana said something about Mary's mom and "Weight Watchers" and how they didn't have "that kind of stuff" for breakfast.

At lunch time, even though she was now starving, she locked herself in a bathroom stall instead of going to the cafeteria. Kids had made snide remarks about her clothes all day, snickering and pointing. One girl who'd never spoken to her before, but today was dressed in all black, said to Mary, "Cool," after looking Mary up and down. *What is she, a Beatnik?* Mary had wondered about the girl.

At last, the bell rang for fifth period. She raced to Miss Boggs's room to find instead an old lady at the head of the class and a sign that said "Mrs. Fairview." Mary's heart sank, and as quickly as it sank, it skipped a beat as she looked into the classroom to see Judy, Maxine, Beverly and Ann huddled together looking as frightened and bewildered as she felt—and wearing clothes that could have come from her own closet.

6

Wake up and Smell the Coffee

"Wake up, sleepy head. I'm headed to get coffee, do you want a coffee or a latte?"

Judy rolled over in bed. She'd slept through her alarm again. She did it almost every morning. She couldn't wait to be an actress and sleep in the day after a big performance. Judy was facing the wall, gazing at Doris Day, but heard her mom stick her head in the doorway. Desi took his opportunity to slip into Judy's room as he did every morning.

"A what?" Since when did Mom allow Judy to drink coffee for breakfast? Or ever? She must have been pretty proud of Judy's performance yesterday in social studies. Judy had told her all about it last night. She still was on cloud nine this morning.

"Up and at 'em, Jujube," said Mrs. White now heading down the hall.

Judy yawned and looked up at James Dean, who smiled down at her approvingly. She looked at Marilyn Monroe and Natalie Wood, happy to have all three of them (she secretly thought of them as friends, though after yesterday at the five-and-dime, she was feeling a little relieved that she could consider real people her friends now).

"By the way," her mom hollered from somewhere in the house (probably the kitchen), "don't forget that you're on your own for dinner tonight. I'm going out with Roger."

Judy started. "Roger? Roger who?" She went to her door, interrupting her morning beauty routine of brushing her hair one hundred times. She lost count; she'd have to start over.

"Oh, let's not do this again. Roger Streeter."

"*Mister* Streeter? Your *boss*?" Judy said with alarm.

"Yes, my boss. I told you, I don't want to have this conversation again. I know it's hard for you to understand, but he makes me happy. And he likes you a lot and that's important to me. I hope you will give him a chance and I bet you will grow to like him."

Judy looked at Desi, who was lounging on her bed, cleaning himself lazily. He looked up at her. "When have we had 'this conversation' before?" she whispered at the cat. He returned all his attention to his right paw, offering her no answer.

Judy pulled from her closet her black and white poodle skirt and her pink angora sweater set. She thought of Bob. Maybe she would catch a glimpse of him at lunch. She would have to make a point of being seen by him today.

"If you don't want a latte or a mocha, I'll just go straight to work," called out Judy's mom. "Don't be late for school!"

"OK, have a good day," Judy responded. She must be groggy. She could barely understand half of what her mom was saying. It sounded like *lahtayn moka*. She started brushing her hair again and now Dragnet pushed the door open and joined the party.

Finally she was dressed and ready. Sometimes she snuck a little of her mom's leftover coffee after she'd gone to work. Before making her way to the kitchen for breakfast, she kissed the top of her autograph book, like she did every morning, and sashayed into the hall. But she stopped dead in her tracks in the living room. The walls were a raspberry color and the sofa was black leather. Across from the sofa was a large black panel on the wall. The phone rang and she jumped about three feet into the air.

She went into the kitchen and reached for the phone, but there was no cord. She stood holding it, staring in disbelief and heard her mother's voice.

"Jujube? Are you there?" The voice came from the device in Judy's hand. She held it to her head.

"Hello?" she said anxiously.

"I didn't want to get off on the wrong foot this morning about Roger. I'm sorry," her mom said.

Certainly she wasn't at work yet, Judy thought. "Where are you?"

"I'm in the car almost to Starbucks. Did you change your mind about a latte?"

In the car? Weirdsville! "No, I don't need a . . . *laytay*. I–Mom, when did we redo the living room?"

"See, I knew it. We should have gone with the Playful Pansy on the walls instead of the Magenta Margarita. You're tired of it already, aren't you?"

"No, it's . . . fine." Judy was starting to be worried that she had gone round the bend. Or her mother had. Or both.

"I've got another call. Call me if you need anything. Love you! Bye!" and her mom had clicked off.

Judy ran back into her room and slammed the door. The cats looked at her in dismay. She never wanted to leave her room. Everything in there was as it always had been. She grabbed her autograph book and held it against her heart. She took one, two, three deep breaths. She gazed at the pictures on the wall, all staring happily at her. She already felt better, and just stood for several moments in silence until the phone rang again.

She dashed to the kitchen once more, trying not to look at her surroundings and grabbed the "phone."

"Jujube, what are you still doing home? I had a feeling you hadn't left for school yet. You're going to be late!"

School would be a welcome relief. She couldn't wait to cut out of her own house.

"Well, don't you look cute?" said Gloria Marshall as she glided into the kitchen.

Maxine almost didn't notice Mama's comment, or the fact that she wasn't already at work, as she was looking around the kitchen. Something was different. Actually, everything was *very* different. The cabinets were painted dark brown, instead of white like they were yesterday. Maxine strained to remember seeing the kitchen upon coming home after being with the girls at the soda fountain; had her Daddy, Uncle TJ and cousin Conrad painted the kitchen? And if so, how did her mama allow it? She loved her immaculately clean white metal cabinets and shiny white walls. And the walls, now they were a dramatic dusty dark green. Even the things on the counter were different; gone was the large cookie jar shaped like an apple. Replacing it was a glossy framed photo of a colored man in a suit and a tie with the American flag behind him. She was about to ask who he was but her attention snapped immediately to her mama when she suggested Maxine looked "cute."

Every morning, Maxine wore blue jean dungarees, penny loafers and a t-shirt, and every morning, her mother demanded she dress like a proper lady the family could be proud of. "Your sister is in one of the finest colleges and we will not have our family disgraced by a greaser daughter! How will you follow in her footsteps if you don't even take pride in your appearance? Do you not realize how many years the Lord has been preparing this family and you think you can just throw it away–" were just some of the arguments that her mother warmed up with.

Maxine knew she should give up and wear the dresses and skirts that Mama, her Auntie, and the Ladies Church Auxiliary sewed for her, but she was a modern woman. Well, determined to be. She was not a stuffed shirt! Besides, if her mother knew what girls wore at her sister's Melba's college, she might be surprised. Maxine imagined the beatnik cool cats in their shades and leather jackets, surrounded by books, discussing philosophy and the arts. She couldn't wait for college and prayed to the dear Lord every night that He would allow her to follow in her sister's footsteps. She knew it was a lot to ask; no man in her family had ever been to college, never mind the fact that she was colored in addition to being a girl. But Melba had done it, and she would too.

As soon as Maxine would protest to Mama, her daddy would reprimand her sharply for crossing her mother's wishes, but when Gloria turned to finish preparing breakfast, John Marshall would wink at his baby and usually Maxine won the day and wore her rolled up blue jeans to school after all.

So this morning, in this strange kitchen, to hear her mother say she looked "cute" was almost too much.

"Do you want me to wear a dress today, Mama?" Maxine volunteered.

"For what, baby?" Mrs. Marshall asked. Maxine turned to see her mother in blue jeans and a long shirt with a wild pattern on it. It almost looked like someone's fancy pajamas! Maxine wondered why she wasn't dressed for the day in her uniform and already on the first of the three buses she took to the Johnsons across town. She realized she'd never even seen Mama in jeans before. She really got to wondering when her daddy came into the kitchen in a suit and a tie!

"Is it Sunday?" Maxine asked reflexively.

Daddy laughed. "I know I'm the only one who wears a suit when I go in, but as soon as I'm promoted, maybe I'll at least lose the tie."

"You'll do no such thing," smiled Mrs. Marshall, kissing her husband.

"Get promoted?" he said.

"Lose the tie!" laughed Gloria, swatting him with a towel.

Maxine gaped at her parents. They were practically giddy, acting like teenagers. They had flipped their lids! Here they were necking in the kitchen like she wasn't even there!

She'd only ever seen her father wearing a suit on Sunday for church. But now here he stood before her looking more proud than she remembered even yesterday, in a blue suit with lapels and pinstripes and no name embroidered on the shoulder like there was on the blue jumpsuit he usually wore.

Staring down at her dry toast, Maxine was suddenly not hungry. She felt as though she had been dropped into a science fiction novel, an alternate universe! *Don't have a cow,* she told herself.

She reached to the tiny gold cross Daddy had gotten her when she was twelve that had hung on a chain around her neck every day since.

"I might need Your help today," she prayed silently.

7

Going, Going, Gone . . .

Ann felt a rush of temporary joy–almost the same feeling that she got whenever she caught a glimpse of the dreamy James O'Grady–when she ran smack-dab into Beverly Jenkins in the hall that morning.

They both started babbling at once.

"Am I glad to see you!" sputtered Ann.

"I think I'm going crazy!" shrieked Beverly.

It was right before second period and Ann had rounded a corner on her way to math, having just come from history, where they had discussed the 1960s . . . *the future . . . as though it had already happened.* In case her morning at home hadn't been kooky enough! She even had to leave her hat in her locker because she got so many strange looks in class. She always wore her sailor hat or her gondolier hat and now besides feeling out of place, she also felt, well, naked.

And there was Beverly, a sight for sore eyes with her usual crooked ponytail and letterman's sweater and tennis shoes. She looked as panicked as Ann felt.

"You mean it's not just me," Ann said.

"I'm having a cow!" Beverly hissed, trying to keep her voice down, even though kids bustling past them gave them no notice. Hours ago, those same kids had looked Beverly up and down like she was from another planet. Ann knew the feeling.

"Was my mom at your house this morning?" Ann asked, hoping for a report. She had nothing but a note from her parents and an oddly different little brother to wake up to.

"No, that's just it! She doesn't work *for* us anymore . . . she works *with* my mom!"

"What?" screeched Ann.

"Cut the gas!" Beverly demanded in a stage whisper. "I'm tired of being stared at all day."

"You?! I had to take my *hat* off!" Ann said dramatically.

"OK, OK, don't go ape. We've got to figure out what's going on here. Is this your nightmare or mine?"

"That's just it, Bev. I don't think this is a dream at all."

Beverly normally ate with her teammates, but upon eyeballing Diane Dunkelman in the hall, she knew she couldn't stomach Diane's antics today. She agreed to meet Ann for lunch, assuming the cafeteria was in the same place, and looked forward to fifth period to see Maxine, Judy and Mary as well. If they weren't the people she thought she knew, well, then . . . all was lost.

"Maxine is 'one of us'!" said Ann, having come from her art class with Maxine, who unfortunately had a later lunch period. She grabbed Beverly's arm. Ann had been waiting by the large entrance to the cafeteria, trying to remain invisible to everyone while she searched for Beverly. Just then, they heard what sounded like the wail of a very sick cat as Judy hurled herself at them.

Before they could take stock of her, Judy was gasping, "How is Bob? Is he alright?"

Alarmed, Beverly said, "Why? What happened?"

"Everything . . . I mean, everything is different. It's all . . . *wrong*! I can't explain it and you wouldn't understand!" Judy whimpered. Judy's heightened drama forced Ann to scale her own sense of calamity down.

"*We* wouldn't understand?" Ann said, gesturing at her clothes and Beverly's.

"Oh!" Judy exclaimed, taking them in for the first time, looking them up and down with big eyes.

"Alright, alright," whispered Beverly. "*You* might dig the attention, but let's just keep it moving and try to keep a low profile as we figure this out." She was going to have to treat this as a big game, the biggest—and she would be team captain. And if she were team captain, this team was not going to lose!

The girls were being bustled into the lunch line by the wave of a hungry crowd.

"I don't have a lunch or any lunch money!" Ann realized suddenly.

"Don't worry, my mom left me ten dollars."

"*Ten dollars!*" Ann and Judy gaped at Beverly in unison.

"Is that for the whole month?" Judy asked.

"For the whole family?" Ann added.

"Maybe," Beverly mused, "maybe I'm supposed to share with my brothers." She cast an eyeball around the cafeteria to look for Bob or Gary.

At the mention of Beverly's brothers, Judy's attention snapped once again to Bob. "Did you see him this morning, Bev? Is he . . . you know . . . *like us?*"

Beverly had gone over her morning a thousand times, but no detail had changed and she still felt queasy. Now standing in the hot lunch line didn't help settle her stomach.

All she could say to Judy was, "Not really."

Like every other morning, Beverly's alarm had rung for nearly a full two minutes before she woke up. Living with rowdy brothers had caused her to become a deep sleeper. At last, she had reached out lazily and swiped at her clock. It was still dark out; she had to get up early to be first in the bathroom and if she wanted to get a run in, she had to rouse herself even earlier. She had stretched her legs, but stayed warm under the covers for a moment longer.

She had gazed at her favorite pennant: the last All-Star team of the All-American Girls Professional Baseball League and felt the lump of her bat against her hip. Always inspired by her "girls," she had gotten up, stretching as she usually did, and performed twenty jumping jacks to get her blood flowing. Putting her yellow terry cloth robe on, her eye had caught a glimpse of her letterman's sweater lying on a chair and her mind had leapt for no logical reason to Conrad Jackson, Maxine's cousin. She had instantly put him out of her thought, but it had taken a great deal of effort. If anything, the effort had been to *want* to put him out of her mind. He appeared in her thoughts and dreams quite often without her permission. When she allowed herself to think about him, she told herself it was his athleticism that she admired and nothing more. (Although she wondered why it would be that when he flashed a smile at her once last fall she felt like her bones had instantly evaporated; was that because he had broken the school record for most stolen bases in a season?) Anyway, it wasn't something her parents would approve of; she had a hard enough time playing sports as she did and depriving her mother of a "ladylike" daughter without adding colored boyfriend to the list.

With that sad thought, her last moment of peace was dashed. She had opened her bedroom door and made her way to the bathroom down the hall. The door had been slightly ajar and she had started as she pushed it open and gazed inside; it was a room she had never seen before! She had jumped back and looked down the hall. There was her bedroom door, and here, eight steps away was supposed to be the bathroom . . .

"It's too early, Bev," her brother Gary, a junior at her school, had groaned. She had recognized his voice but been unable to see his face as he was a lump under a pile of covers on a bed that was in a room that hadn't been there yesterday. She had been fixed to the spot, her mind racing. Gary had tossed a pillow at the door to close it, but missed. The pillow had fallen at her feet.

Then she could move . . . she had backed slowly down the hall, one step gingerly behind the other, and hesitantly pushed on the door across from her room. It had been a bathroom alright, but not one she had ever seen! There were four sinks; two along one side of the wall and two more directly across from them. Next to those, a door on each side, and beyond that a separate room with a toilet and a shower. The only thing she had been able to think to do was to step inside and touch something to see if it was real.

If this had been a dream, Conrad would have been central to it and she'd have been holding his hand walking in the park, or playing catch with him, or at a Cardinals game together . . .

She had spotted a white towel draped by one of the sinks. "Bev," the hot pink monogram read. She had noticed other towels then, some hanging cockeyed, some wadded on the floor, one tossed over the shower curtain. They had been monogrammed, too, but with her brother's names.

"Sink or shower?"

She had flinched. The voice behind her had become two strong hands that grabbed her by her shoulders to move her to the side.

"Morning. Sink or shower?" her older brother Jerry Jr. had repeated. He had looked different. Beverly had noticed at once his flat top hair seemed much longer. He had just come in from a run and the smell of chilly spring air and sweat, mingling, caused a strange steam to rise off of him.

"Hello? Are you awake yet?"

"Uh, sink," Beverly had muttered.

"Cool." Jerry Jr. had moved into the room with the toilet and shower, pulling the pocket door closed behind him.

As the shower burst on behind the closed door, Beverly had taken what she presumed to be her towel and pressed it to her face. Her heart had begun to thud heavily, uncomfortably, and she felt hot. She had turned one of the faucets on at a dribble, so as not to overheat Larry's shower, and patted her face with the shockingly cold water. But she did not feel better. Her toothbrush had gone missing and she had picked up a thick heavy toothbrush-looking item that had a button on it. It had started buzzing in her hand and made her involuntarily exclaim, "Oh!" She had dropped the thing, rubbed some toothpaste on her teeth with her index finger and darted out of the bathroom. She had wanted to be gone before Larry came back out, and dashed to her room, slamming the door behind her.

In her room, everything had been normal and as it should be. There were her pennants, there was her crumpled bed. She was grateful for her own space; she was the only one in the family who didn't share a room. She had thought briefly of climbing back into bed, but instead went and pulled the covers tightly across it, smoothing out any wrinkles or creases and leaning her Louisville Slugger against the wall next her bed. How many times had her mother told her to make her bed in the morning and she never did it (but always found it made when she came home from school)? Couldn't she at least do this for her mother?

With her mother in mind, she had hurriedly dressed and went to find her. As she pulled her letterman's sweater around her shoulders, she had heard her mother call out, "There's a granola bar and lunch money! I'm leaving early again!" and below Beverly, the front door had closed.

Beverly had flown out of her bedroom and to the staircase, her feet not even touching the stairs as she dashed after her mom. She had moved with such speed, she hadn't noticed her surroundings at first. But when she had determined that she had missed her mother, she had begun to take in the scene. The living room space had appeared to be theirs alright, but the colors were different, the furniture looked strangely boxy . . . and there on the wall was a large portrait of the family; all seven of them smiling happily as if everything were normal. Beverly had run to the picture hoping for some clue or comfort. They were all wearing white oxford shirts, Beverly's hair in a pony tail as always. Beverly's mother's hair looked unusually bushy; in fact everyone else's hair looked odd—loose and long and coarse. Beverly had backed away from the portrait and found herself in the kitchen. How long would it be before Mrs. B came? Probably still at least two hours, she had figured. Then she had caught a glimpse of a note attached to the fridge (and even the fridge looked different!).

Bev,
Can't take you to school this morning. Please get a ride from one of the boys. Kat and I are finishing our presentation and giving our bid today! Cross your fingers! Dad's at the store early for training.
Love you,
Mom

Beverly had sighed with relief at the mention of Pops and the store. *At least he still had the hardware store . . . something was normal. Now who was Kat?* Even as she thought it, she had realized Kat must be Katrina Branislav, Mrs. B.

Presentation? Bid? Did her mother *have a job?*

Beverly had wandered back into the kitchen in a daze, clutching her letterman's sweater, the only familiar thing, close to her. She had gingerly reached for the cabinet near the sink to get herself a cereal bowl, but touched the handle as if it were radioactive. She didn't know how long she stood and stared into space, but eventually, Jerry Jr. had come bounding in, rubbing his wet hair with a towel.

"You need a lift?" he had asked, not noticing how strange, upside down and backwards the universe had become.

Without thinking, Beverly had nodded yes and with that she had jumped onto the speeding train that was to become the rest of her day.

Having found each other at lunch, Judy, Ann and Beverly didn't want let go of each other and looked forward to fifth period where they hoped to also find Maxine and Mary. Mary was the brains; she'd better have an explanation for all this!

Sure enough, when they entered social studies, there sat Maxine with a look of determined pride. She held herself with confidence, but her frightened eyes told another story. The girls quickly gathered around her, filling vacant seats nearby and asking about her day. With their whispers they tried to be discreet, but failed miserably. Their clothes had been drawing unwanted attention all day and now that they were grouped together, it was even worse. There was snickering and outright pointing and laughing.

Kids streamed in the door and many were already in class. Finally, Mary entered the classroom and a mixture of dread and euphoria bubbled up in her. She spotted her four friends waiting for her and relished the moment when the final bell would ring and the whispers and openly snide comments would come to a halt. She silently crossed herself, using great restraint to not drop to her knees in gratitude at the sight of the other girls or out of utter confusion and exhaustion from her morning.

Miss Boggs was nowhere to be seen. In fact, on the teacher's desk was a plaque that read "Mrs. Fairview." An older silver-haired lady hunched over a lesson plan gave the girls a curious glance and went back to her book until the class started. With a flicker of panic, each of the girls vaguely registered Miss Boggs's absence, noting that all her other teachers had been the same as before, except with modern hair and clothes.

Bev, Judy, Maxine and Ann watched Mary enter the classroom. They'd reserved the desk behind Beverly and Mary slid in behind her. Beverly seemed uncharacteristically frail, clutching her books to her chest. When Mary gave her an encouraging pat on the shoulder, Beverly loosened her grip on the books and laid them clumsily on her desk top, but the top book slipped and dropped to the floor with a sharp crack, just missing a large tennis-shoed foot.

A strong dark-skinned hand swooped down and retrieved the book smoothly, placing it squarely on her desk. Beverly looked up to see Conrad's beautiful brown eyes twinkling at her. Involuntarily, she breathed, "Golly . . ." as he made his way past her to a desk in the back.

The bell rang and someone from the corner of the room said "Golly!" in a mocking falsetto and the class exploded into laughter. Beverly slunk into her spot feeling an uncomfortable heat rise in her cheeks. She felt feverish, queasy . . . and something else not quite so terrible . . . .

One thing was for sure: she was a goner. In more ways than one.

8

No News is Bad News

Ann stretched and yawned. She had obviously slept or she wouldn't be waking up, but she felt exhausted. She had the strangest dream last night that seemed to go on forever and a day. Looking around her room, which was no bigger than a large closet accommodating a bed, dresser, and an easel for painting, she felt a trace of comfort that was enough to ease some of the fatigue. It *was* all a dream, she reassured herself. A very detailed, weird, crazy dream . . . but it *must* have been a dream. She spotted Bubbe's paintbrush on her easel a few steps away and sighed with relief.

Her thoughts went to Bev and the Jenkins' family business. In her dream, she and the girls from social studies had been thrown into the future–fifty-five years into the future, they figured (just like their Travel to Tomorrow project!). After a kooky day at school, the gals decided to meet at the five-and-dime for a malt to try to straighten the whole mess out (Mary's idea . . . she said they would "retrace their steps" like Nancy Drew would do).

Only when they got to the five-and-dime, it was a parking lot. And not only was the drugstore gone, Bev's Pops's hardware store was gone! Bev had looked green and they had to steady her while she wobbled on her feet.

Ann shuddered at the memory, and though she knew she was being silly, she hopped out of bed and opened her door to look down the short hall of her house. All the uneasy feelings of her dream flooded back as she caught a glimpse of the living room. Drat it all anyway, she was still dreaming . . . or being dreamed . . . or . . . something like that.

Ann leaned against the doorjamb and tried to get her bearings so she wouldn't feel so dizzy. She heard a light tapping sound from the living room and curiosity got the best of her. She recovered and tiptoed the few steps to the living room and spotted her mother—or rather, the new version of her mother—curled up on the sofa typing on a flat keyboard in her lap. A shaft of lavender morning light lit one side of Mrs. Branislav, and the rest of the room remained in grainy shadow. For just a moment, Ann could imagine in this dim lighting that she was in the home she knew again; but an eerie glow from the device that was on her mother's lap destroyed her hopeful musings. Her mother's long brown locks, usually wrapped in a tidy bun under a head scarf to show she was a good, God-fearing orthodox Jewish woman, now hung short and loose, tucked behind one ear, falling forward as she leaned toward her lap. Her feminine features looked sharp in the harsh light.

Ann assumed her little brother Alex was still sleeping, while her dad, her *tatty*, must have already left for the factory. He worked the early shift to be home when she and Alex returned from school in the afternoons, since her mom always helped

Mrs. Jenkins with dinner. Her tatty was a man of few words but the kindest, gentlest soul she had ever known. She'd never seen him angry or agitated. Whenever Ann had a problem, she would weigh what kind of a response she needed. If it was a hug and reassurance, it was straight to her father. If it was guts and inspiration to take action, she went to her mom. Little Alex took after his tatty; he was quiet and thoughtful and hardly ever stirred up trouble. But even they were different in this new world, in ways that Ann couldn't place. A sharpness, or a sense of rushing, a distracted air. A carelessness had seemed to replace the resident melancholy. Seeing them yesterday after she got home from her meeting with the other girls hadn't been as comforting as she'd hoped. They were just different enough that it was unsettling.

The most disconcerting thing that Ann discovered was the one set of silverware, and all plates and cups housed together in one cabinet: her mother wasn't keeping Kosher! Ann had sometimes felt guilty for secretly resenting living in a Kosher household: the inconvenience, the laborious ritualism, the oddness-to-the-rest-of-the-world of it (all of which she knew, of course, was the whole point). But she hadn't realized how much of her identity it really was. Now she was painfully conscious of her new *traif* existence, and instead of feeling liberated, she felt adrift.

Against her better judgment, but feeling the need to be close to her mother, Ann went to sit against her on the sofa.

"Morning, darling," Mrs. Branislav said, kissing the top of Ann's head while her fingers kept tapping away. Ann's small white dog, Meshuga, a sleeping puffball on the other side of Ann's mother, thumped a lazy good morning with her tail.

"What are you doing?" Ann asked, gazing at what looked like a small shallow TV screen attached to the flat typewriter her mother typed on.

"Up early to finish this proposal. Look, Margie's up, too." She pointed to the screen, where there was a small outlined square where words kept popping up. As Mrs. Branislav spoke, a line appeared out of nowhere that read,

5toLove: LOL, Kat. It can't hurt! ;~)

Ann rubbed her eyes. The light from the tiny screen was so bright. Her mother chuckled softly. "I told Margie that we've got an advantage since Jerry is the manager." Ann relished in the sound of her mother's voice, one of the few things that hadn't changed in this backwards world. It still sounded like music, with her Slavic accent just barely influencing her words. Ann was happy to be American, but wished she had a romantic-sounding accent like her mother that hinted at far-off lands, foreign adventures and deep family roots.

Ann, wanting to understand what was happening and also wanting to hear more of her mother's voice, asked, "Mama, what is it that you're working on?"

"Margie's and my company put a bid in to be the cleaning company for Home Pro and we met with them yesterday. Of course Jerry was at the meeting since he's the store manager, so I think we have the advantage. They just needed some additional numbers, so I'm going to email them over this morning. We should know very soon if we got the job!"

The words "Home Pro" sparked something in Ann's memory from yesterday. "Oh!" she gasped. "Home Pro is the big store . . . ."

"The home improvement store over on Third Street, darling. Where Mr. Jenkins is the manager," Mrs. Branislav reminded her while she typed and words came up on the screen,

KatKleans: I'll email final #s now if u approve.

It suddenly became clear to Ann: "Margie" and "Jerry" were Mrs. and Mr. Jenkins. Her mother no longer worked *for* them, she worked *with* Mrs.–er, *Margie* Jenkins. And instead of owning a hardware store, Mr. Jenkins now managed that monstrous warehouse-looking place called Home Pro that rose like a mighty cinderblock cube out of the asphalt plane of a parking lot that lay where Jenkins Hardware used to be only days ago. *Poor Beverly*. Ann needed to let her know right away! Though she hated to leave her mother's side, she tore herself away to get ready for school and go find Bev.

"Did you need the computer, darling?" Ann's mother called after her.

"Uh, no thanks, Mom. I'm cool."

But she wasn't cool. *Computer*? It was official. They had arrived in the future.

Choosing her clothes carefully so as not to get the gawks she got yesterday, Ann selected her least conspicuous gray pedal-pushers, her white top and a light pink cardigan sweater and tied a white scarf around her head. She debated bringing her paint-brush with her to school, as she was sorry to leave the safe confines of her sweet little room and its familiar contents. But not wanting to lose the brush, and eager to find Bev, she left it and closed the door behind her protectively as she left.

Dear Diary,   6th of May

    Day 2 of The Case of the Long Weird Dream. I've been gathering clues, but the more I know the less I know. Danny, Patty and Maggie are the same. Except for being totally different. It's like the book, Invasion of the Body Snatchers . . . they have the same bodies but they're louder (I sure didn't know that was possible!), do whatever they want and run wild like banshees! Mother and Nana seem different, too. There's no discipline in this whole house, none! I'm the only one with any sense. Which is what worries me . . . I wonder if I'm the one who's been snatched!!

    I don't know what I would do without the girls. Today after school we went to the five-and-dime; I think it's the scene of the crime—that moment with Miss Boggs the day of the presentation? I have a funny feeling about it . . . .

    But the five-and-dime is totally gone, along with Jenkins Hardware. You can only imagine Bev's face. Broke my heart. Judy as usual, forgetting all about Bev, even though she's standing right in front of her face, starts flipping out about Bob! I don't even know if Bob knows that doll exists, her life and our lives are turned upside down, and she swoons over that boy. I gave her a look like, "Cut the gas! Think about Bev just once!" She didn't even see me. Sometimes I wonder about that girl's jets!

We hung at a coffee shop instead. I don't mean a diner kind of joint, it was a whole store of just coffee. A cup was 4 bucks! Who has that kind of bread to pay four dollars for a cup of joe? Mother and Nana drink coffee like it's water . . . . In fact, Mother doesn't smoke now and drinks coffee instead!

And speaking of family, I think mine are all off their rockers. I heard Mother on the phone with Daddy like having a phone conversation with him was no big deal. For five years, she wouldn't talk about him, and now out of the clear blue sky, it's just peachy that he ditched his ankle-biters. I thought I heard Mother say that we'd be seeing him this weekend! That's more than I can take. I'll keep you in orbit . . . if I survive any of this. Until then, I am as
Always ?
Mary
PS- My pink circle skirt got some eyeballs, but not the kind I want!
PPS- Miss Boggs is missing. She's the only teacher that is gone . . . all the rest are the same! I have a bad feeling about this! Our new social studies teacher is an old lady named Mrs. Fairview.
PPPS- Danny, Patty or Maggie: I know this won't do any good, but - **Stop reading my diary!**

This will make a great novel. I will ride the rails, hop in a convertible and cruise the Interstate here in the future and write my observations. I will find the other artists, musicians, poets and writers who have found their voice and we will rap for hours in dusky roadside coffeehouses across the country. I will live adrift on my dreams, forever free . . . .

I just keep telling myself this is all very romantic.

If only I believed it.

Great Grandma worked on a cotton plantation as a slave when she was younger and when I was a little girl, I couldn't understand why she wasn't miserable or disappointed with her life. She told Mama, "Glo, when everybody know they place, everybody happy." I never understood how that could be so.

Until now.

—M.E.M.

Dear Diary,   May 6

I am still scared . . . and a little sad for my friend Beverly. Today all of us girls went to Woolworths for a soda and to talk about our, you know, situation. I for one was hoping Mary would have some illuminations! (She didn't.) But just like everything else, our whole town is different! Mr. Jenkins's hardware store is missing! I felt crushed for Beverly, Diary, just crushed. She probably feels like I do right now. See, Mom is dating her boss! I don't know what happened to Daddy, but I wish he was here. In 1950, when we got the news that he died in Korea, we were a real mess. But here and now, Mom is over it and playing backseat bingo with Mr. Streeter for all I know! The only good thing about all this, Diary, is that Bob is fine, just fine. I saw him after school and he even cast me an eyeball, looked right at me! My knees felt wobbly and my throat went dry. Even though his hair is different, he is still dreamy. (His hair is longer, but he doesn't have any VO5 in it, it's just loose and dry looking.) Oh, Diary, when he looked at me, it's like I didn't even care that everything was kooky. He gave me a strange look, but at least it was a look. Maybe all this will be worth it if he asks me out on a date and someday I can wear his jacket or put his class ring on a necklace around my neck.

Still Real Gone,

♡ ~~Judy White~~ – Mrs. Robert Jenkins –
Mrs. Judy Jenkins – J. E. J

I don't know what I would do without athletics. I take all that lost feeling, all that frustration with that Diane Dunkelman, all the funny looks, and pour it into my game. Today after school, I discovered that Pops's store is no more. I wanted to kick or hit something, but there were no balls around, only people. So after saying good-bye to Maxine, Mary, Judy and Ann, I walked back to school. The sun was setting and the boys were done with baseball practice, but there were still some bats and balls around. I picked up a bat, stood at home plate and tossed some balls in the air. When the bat connected, hearing that crack and the ball whistle through the air, I didn't care what year it is, I felt like myself. After 4 or 5 balls went over the back fence, Coach Riggins, the boy's coach, called my name. I thought I was alone. "Jenkins!" he called me. I jumped and turned to see him grinning at me. All he said was, "You wanna try out for my team before Saturday's game?" and I said, "Yes, sir!" Boy, my heart was pounding fast then. I can't wait to play with the boys. Oh, I mean if I get on the team…

Bev

6 May

Dear Irina,

I have only your old letters and nothing new. I am concerned that something terrible has happened to you, to your father. My family is not the same. My mother is no longer a maid! We no longer keep Kosher. For all I know, we're not even Jewish any more. For the second day now, I am trying to sort through what has become of my life . . . and yours! So that I don't go crazy, I will tell you the things that are the same: the daffodils are blooming in the glorious color of the spring sun; the boy I told you about, James O'Grady, still has the keenest green eyes; and . . . the girls I did my school project with. They are exactly the same. A few nights ago we met to say good-bye, but now it feels as though we are bound together. They are my biggest comfort and maybe my only hope.

—Ann

Mary was beside herself . . . tonight her father was taking her and the kids out to dinner. She hadn't seen him in two years (or was it *fifty*-two years?). She wasn't capable of sounding peachy keen with him like her mom was on the phone. Besides, even though school was mostly terrifying, at least she was starting to get used to it since her yesterday seemed infernally long. And she had fifth period to look forward to when she'd see the other girls. She tried to ignore the horrible possibility that one of the girls—or all of them—would become like everybody else and decide that it was Mary who was off her rocker.

She slid into the desk in front of Judy before class started. Mrs. Fairview, flipping through her syllabus at the head of the class, caught Mary's eye. Mary felt a strange kinship with Mrs. Fairview and they smiled at each other, but Mrs. Fairview quickly looked away. For the briefest moment, Mary longed to tell Mrs. Fairview about their dilemma, but immediately buried the urge. What would Mrs. Fairview think of that, and more importantly, how would it negatively impact Mary's current events grade? (Mary had been surprised to learn that social studies was now called current events. Her new favorite subject was math, because it was the only thing that hadn't changed. Which was saying a lot because she really despised math.)

Judy leaned over Mary's shoulder. "Am I glad to see you! I asked the others if they want to come over tonight. Can you come?"

There was nothing . . . well, almost nothing . . . Mary wanted more. "I have to go to dinner with my dad tonight," she said with a catch in her throat.

"Your dad?" Judy was surprised. "Did you used to . . . *before* . . . ?"

Mary shook her head no.

"I think our parents have gone ape!" Judy said, thinking of her mother and her mother's new boyfriend.

"How about you?" Mary whispered. "Have you found out anything about your father?"

Now Judy shook her head no, with a heaviness in her heart. Even her perky blonde pigtails didn't look perky. She knew her father must still be dead, but knew even less about the circumstances than she did before.

As the bell rang, Beverly, disheveled, lunged to her desk with papers trailing behind her. Her grace and coordination seemed limited to the playing field. She glanced at somebody at the back of the room before quickly lowering her eyes. Judy and Mary both gave her a questioning look, but before Bev could explain her reasons for being flustered, not the least of which included her tryout tomorrow, Mrs. Fairview started class.

"I always ask: who wants to earn extra credit? Anyone read any news stories they want to share?"

Chuck Spaunhorst, ever the greaser, without raising his hand, called out, "More US troops were killed in the Middle East."

Mrs. Fairview, not willing to give extra credit without a little more to go on, said, "Are you just stating the obvious, or did you read something about it and have more to share?"

Chuck shrugged his shoulders and slumped in his chair, resigned to the "D" he was mostly likely going to see on his report card at the end of the semester.

Encouraging the class, and using Chuck's comment as a starting off point, Mrs. Fairview said, "What do we know about what's going on in the Middle East?"

Mary's mind began spinning. The last she knew, the US and several other countries were trying to defend against Soviet expansion in the Middle East. Iraq had just signed a treaty with Turkey a few months back, in February 1955. Feeling excited that she might be putting some pieces together, Mary uncharacteristically said without being called on, "Is there a war with the Soviets?"

There was a strange hush in the room and a few snickers. Mrs. Fairview's face wrinkled up in a funny way and she searched for the right words to gently break the news to Mary that there were no more Soviets because the Soviet Union had broken up.

Mary's mouth dropped open, as did Maxine's and Ann's.

"Oh," Mary squeaked.

Mrs. Fairview's expression grew concerned, and she seemed almost as anxious as Mary. "You're not in trouble, Mary, but I'd like to see you after class," Mrs. Fairview said, but her attention quickly shifted: "Conrad! What did I say about texting in my classroom? Put the phone away, or it's mine."

While Bev listened to Conrad get scolded for something she didn't understand, a familiar buzzing sound filled Mary's ears. *No more Soviets! Was the Cold War over? Was Communism dead?*

Ann had the same questions, wondering how it fit in with the fact that Yugoslavia was no more.

Maxine wondered at her cousin, Conrad. She had never seen him get scolded in class before.

Judy hoped they could all come to her house tonight and straighten this whole thing out, maybe find some updated clothes to wear . . . or, at the very least, commiserate together.

9

It Ain't Like it Used to Be

"I know you're working hard and thinking about extra credit," Mrs. Fairview said, keeping her eyes down at the syllabus on her desk, "but if you don't know the answers, you don't need to *always* speak up."

Mary's face burned red. Mrs. Fairview's next class was beginning to trickle in. The words smarted, no matter how delicately Mrs. Fairview attempted to deliver them, and Mary felt unfairly reprimanded. She shifted her books, wishing she could vanish. Talking to Mrs. Fairview was worse than making a fool of herself in class.

Her teacher glimpsed Mary's pained expression before she turned to leave. "Mary . . . " Mrs. Fairview's voice softened, which only made Mary want to cry more. "It's going to be OK." Her voice was full of meaning, but Mary didn't know what she meant. She nodded sharply and rushed out of the room to her next class.

In Maxine's seventh period history class, Mr. Steinberg was giving his version of World War II. It was his version, Maxine felt, because she had actually *lived* through it as a child. Although she was interested in what he had to say, she felt herself start to mentally drift. She found herself wondering about the man in the picture she'd seen on the kitchen counter. Her parents would think she was loopy if she asked them who he was; he must be a family member or someone close to her family if he had such a place of honor. Mr. Steinberg talked about President Roosevelt's desire to get involved in the conflict in Europe, but the rest of America was slow to come around. Maxine looked up at the picture of President Roosevelt; all the U.S. Presidents had their pictures lining the history classroom and Maxine glanced around at all of them. There was Ike, the man who was president following him, and after them, several more white men . . . and then Maxine gasped and exclaimed, "He's the *President*!"

The other students and Mr. Steinberg turned their attention to Maxine and she shrunk under their stares. As Mr. Steinberg turned her outburst into a contribution to the conversation, she continued to gaze at the portrait on the wall: the colored man in the frame in her kitchen was President of the United States. She could barely catch her breath and didn't hear another word that Mr. Steinberg said for the rest of the class period.

After school, Maxine paced her room excitedly, her great-grandmother's quill in her hand. What did this mean, that a black man was president? Maxine thought of W.E.B. DuBois's words that "the problem of the twentieth century is the problem of the color line." Was the line gone? Had the "problem" come and gone with the twentieth century? Her heart swelled. The future was the *most!* Whatever had happened in the last fifty-five years, it had worked! There was equality at long last and all was well.

But she couldn't ignore a nagging feeling; whenever Conrad came to thought, something didn't fit. If the future was so grand and civil rights had been obtained, why did Conrad seem to have a chip on his shoulder? He was not the cousin she knew—courteous, polite. He was always a lot of fun, but he had never been disrespectful. But now there was a carelessness about him. She'd seen Conrad after school with a group of guys, no better than a gang of greasers, yelling, shoving each other and causing a scene. Even if they were ultimately being playful with each other, they obviously made everyone nearby nervous enough to cause a moat of empty space around them as people avoided them.

As Maxine had looked on, she had clutched her books to her chest, maybe unconsciously for protection, as she stood near the front doors of the school. Conrad noticed her from the parking lot, and hollered out, "Hey, Cuz!"

She couldn't believe she'd done it, but she had pretended she didn't see him and ducked back into the school building, hoping no one would associate her with him. Thoroughly ashamed of herself, she had run to the restroom where she locked herself in a stall to cry in private.

Where she had come from, it seemed like white folks were just waiting for an excuse to fire the colored folks who worked for them, or in some way make their lives more difficult just as a reminder of who really had the power. Maxine knew then, as Conrad did, that you just didn't draw negative attention to your-self for the simple fact that you already *had* attention on yourself–due to the color of your skin. No one in her family was disrespectful or the whole family would pay the price in one way or another. In as big a city as they lived, it was still a small town when it came to the color of your skin.

For so much good news, it was a lot for Maxine to sort through. She thought instantly of her sister Melba and longed to talk with her.

Maxine found her mama in the kitchen, having just walked in and taking off a pair of high-heeled boots. Her hair was cropped close to her head and had its natural tiny curls instead of the big smooth curls her mother had worked so hard to attain before. Once again, she was in jeans and Maxine tried to not raise her eyebrows in surprise. This must mean no more waiting hand and foot on the Johnson family!

They greeted each other with a hug. When Maxine closed her eyes and felt her mama's arms around her, she could pretend for the briefest second that everything was simple. But then she opened her eyes and spotted their strange new kitchen.

"Mama, I want to call Melba," Maxine said, not sure how to go about doing that.

"Now, baby, please don't start on me again for your own phone. I already told you, we don't want to spend our money on it, and you're not getting a job to pay for it because I want you to focus on school to get your scholarships."

Maxine wasn't sure what to say to all that, so she waited. Her mama continued, "Besides, when you gonna use it? We're always going to know where you are, here or at school. And I don't want my daughter using her phone in the middle of class."

Maxine argued, "Well, Conrad does."

"That's my point. Your cousin Conrad is the perfect example. Boy has got to learn some manners, and who's going to teach him? Poor TJ, working day and night with no time to be a good daddy to that boy. And that Mama of his is worse than useless."

Some strange loyalty to the Conrad she knew before bubbled up in Maxine, even as she gazed at the portrait of the President on their kitchen counter.

"Conrad's a good boy, Mama. He tries real hard."

"I know, baby. And you try real hard, too. You want me to warm you up something for supper? Daddy's working late again tonight."

It had never been a question of Mama making dinner. Every night, no matter how late anyone was working, dinner was on the table. And now it was . . . optional. Last night, Mama had brought home buckets of chicken from a restaurant instead of making it herself. Instead of running another family's household, Gloria Marshall ran an office.

"Would it be alright if I went to Judy's tonight?" Maxine asked. She wasn't sure what her mom would think about the late notice and spending more and more time with white girls.

Mama flipped through a pile of bills and said absently, "Of course, baby."

A black man as President, her mother's new job not easing the strain on their family, Conrad's questionable behavior, Maxine's feeling lost and alone; these were not details she'd included in her Travel to Tomorrow predictions.

Maxine thought of Jack Kerouac's words: *All of life is a foreign country.*

Mary waved goodbye–bare-fingered–to her father as he dropped her off on Judy's doorstep. Her white gloves were tucked in her pocket. She had considered it a special occasion and dressed appropriately, but he had actually laughed at her gloves, as had her sisters and brother when they saw her sitting on the davenport by the front door waiting. The little pill box hat with the pink peony hadn't gone over real swiftly, either.

Now at Judy's door, she felt like she could breathe again. At least she'd have some time with the girls.

The door swung open and Ann welcomed Mary in. "We're in Judy's room," she said and before Mary could ask why, she surmised the reason. Judy's house was entirely different than the last time she'd been here. It was the exact opposite, in fact. Instead of white and pale colors, it was bold and dark and felt claustrophobic.

"Have I missed much? Is Mrs. White home?" Mary couldn't stand the thought of everyone as a group, piecing together clues and comparing notes, without her.

Ann shook her head no, and before she opened the door to Judy's room, she whispered scandalously, "Mrs. White is out . . . on a . . . *date!*" The door opened as Mary's mouth made a little "o".

She wanted to weep when she saw her friends in Judy's room. It was completely *normalsville.* Judy's pigtails, Bev's letterman jacket, Maxine's dungarees, and Ann's pedal-pushers, all against the backdrop of Judy's 1950s Hollywood stars-laden walls, felt like a bucket of ice water in the desert.

"Mary!" Judy flew from her spot at her vanity to embrace Mary. Mary felt a tinge of guilt at her latest diary entry about

Judy, but suppressed it to enjoy the moment. Everyone else greeted her just as warmly, and Maxine made space on the bed.

"What have I missed?" Mary asked, adjusting her plaid skirt.

"Oh, nothing, just the last half a century," Maxine joked. They all laughed nervously. Then Maxine told them all what she had discovered about the President.

"Gee, whiz," Ann sighed. "We've come a long way!" The girls all marveled.

"We sure have; and we have greatness right here in this room. Bev is playing *baseball* tomorrow," Judy announced. "With the *boys*! We're all going to go." Judy was jazzed, and though she didn't say it (for once), everyone knew she was just as excited to see Bev play with the boys as she was to see Bob play.

"How are *you* playing with the boys? I know you're good and all, but you're a *girl*," Mary said.

Bev wasn't offended because she knew what Mary meant and, quite honestly, had thought the same thing herself. She explained to Mary, as she already had to the others, that it was only a *tryout*; the boys' coach had been watching her for some time. He'd told her he saw her potential for athletic scholarships and wanted to give her a chance to "show her stuff."

"Golly," Mary sighed, and the others sighed with her as if hearing it for the first time.

"Score one for the future," Bev said, but it sounded more like a question than a statement.

"Score *two* for the future," Maxine added fervently in honor of her discovery. They nodded.

Then all attention turned to Mary as Ann said to her, "Tell us about your dinner with your dad."

Mary felt herself start to blush, and then, by some force of will, she stopped; she had nothing to hide and no reason to feel self-conscious, here of all places. And maybe confiding in them would help. It wasn't something she'd felt safe doing *before* . . . but now . . .

She started in, telling them how she had dressed in her Sunday best, including her gloves and hat, and the girls knew right away where it was going, having gotten all the odd looks themselves.

"The kids," Mary said, referring to her younger siblings, "were in t-shirts, for crying out loud!" Bev and Maxine exchanged a quick look. T-shirts were their preferred wardrobes, but they understood Mary's point: wearing a t-shirt to a family dinner out at a restaurant would never fly where they came from.

"I'm tired of being gawked at." Ann sympathized with Mary about their clothing drawing unwanted attention. "But my clothes and everything in my room is the same while the rest of the world just flew past without me."

The girls nodded in agreement.

"Maybe we should go shopping for new clothes!" Judy's eyes twinkled at the prospect.

"I doubt my mama's going to go for that," Maxine said, knowing that her parents had always been on a very tight budget.

"Mine either," Mary said. She'd been thinking of making herself a new dress anyway; why would she go spend money on new clothes if she had everything she needed to make just what she wanted?

"Well, we need *some* kind of a plan!" Judy said forcefully.

"Instead of shopping for new clothes, maybe we should figure out why the clothes in our closet—and our rooms, but nothing else—came with us," offered Bev.

Mary said, "First, we need to find out if this is even real—"

"Oh, it's real, alright, real *kooky*," Maxine interrupted under her breath.

"We've got to figure out what is happening and why." Mary recovered quickly.

"Who cares about why? I just want to go home," said Ann.

"The *why* could be the key to this whole thing: why us? Why now?" Bev wondered.

"What is happening is just as important . . . did we time travel? Are we in a parallel dimension? Is this a big dream that we're somehow all dreaming?" pondered Maxine out loud.

Judy burst into tears. They all stopped and stared at her.

"I'm sorry," she sobbed. "But this is all so scary. What's even more scary is I don't think I'm smart enough to figure it all out, so I'll probably just be trapped here while you all go on home without me."

Mary put her arms around Judy. "Let's promise each other that if we have anything to say about it, no one goes anywhere—or, uh, any *when*—without all of us."

The girls agreed.

"We need to figure this out in bite-sized pieces," Maxine said thoughtfully.

Mary adjusted her glasses, but kept one arm around Judy. But when she started gesturing enthusiastically, Judy got knocked around a bit. "We'll each take an assignment, like we did with the Travel to Tomorrow project!"

"That turned out well," Ann said sarcastically.

"Well, I think that's where we should start, that project," Bev said. "I volunteer Mary to find out what that class project has to do with our, um, predicament." She straightened her ever-loosening pony tail. Some things never changed.

"That's not a bite-sized piece," Mary argued. "That could be the whole mystery."

Then they all started speaking at once:

"Oh, yeah? Why *is* my room the same, but not the rest of my house?"

"And why aren't we or our families any older, but we're in the future?"

"And why are all of our teachers the same, except for one? Where's Miss Boggs, the person who gave us the assignment?"

"And why are our families the same people, but totally different?"

Once again, the mystery and weight of their plight settled over them.

Mary gazed absently at one of the pictures of James Dean on Judy's wall. She wondered if Judy knew yet that James Dean had died in a tragic car crash just a few months after . . . or years before . . . anyway, in September 1955. Following her talk with Mrs. Fairview, Mary had high-tailed it after school to the library and found a book on 1955 in the reference section. She had felt like she was cheating, but she had read all she could about the final months of the year from which she had been displaced.

Finally, Mary said quietly, "Alright. Bite-sized pieces."

They each volunteered to investigate a piece of the puzzle. Mary would look into whatever had happened to Miss Boggs. Judy would find out about their class project. Bev agreed to investigate why their families were all the same people, but "different." Maxine planned to analyze how it was that no one had aged, yet they were fifty-five years into the future, while Ann was eager to discover why only their rooms and clothes remained intact.

A hush fell over the room as they ruminated on their "bite-sized" chunks, which suddenly didn't feel so bite-sized. More than one of them was ambivalent about solving the riddle, curious if it would mean they would wake up back in 1955. *Of course I want to go home,* Bev thought, *but it's not so awful here....*

They had their assignments. And in the meantime, they'd just have to make the best of it, starting with going to Bev's tryout for the boys' varsity baseball team tomorrow.

10

Round the Bend and Outta the Park

Ann couldn't tell who was more nervous, Beverly or Judy. She sat on the bleachers with Maxine on one side, Mary on the other, and Judy on the end. Once again, Mary had dressed for the occasion with gloves, a little wrap (even though it was seventy-four degrees), and a hat, while Judy wore her favorite poodle skirt and had obviously just polished her saddle shoes. Maxine wore a cotton dress with a white peter pan collar, and Ann had put her hat on to shade herself in the bright sun. Judy was a bundle of energy and couldn't sit still; Beverly in the dugout sat by herself and kept glancing back at her friends.

That is, until Judy kept waving and calling out, "Go Bev! Go Indians!" Then Bev ducked her head and didn't look back.

A few casual observers in the stands chuckled and muttered, "Who are the *Indians*?"

Mary glanced at the scoreboard, adjusting her glasses. "I don't think we're the Indians anymore, we're the . . . well, one of those . . ." She pointed a gloved finger toward the scoreboard which featured the word **Rams** in bold script. Little did the girls realize that it had been years since a group of folks realized that the cartoon Indian mascot was offensive and their new school mascot was a now a scowling Ram.

Judy seemed deflated. "Golly," she said, but quickly recovered when she caught sight of Bob. He'd gone to his sister, said a few words and then gone back to sit with the two other guys the coach had called to help with the tryout. She thought she spotted Maxine's cousin. Peeling her eyes off of Bob for just a second, she glanced around. "Where are Mr. and Mrs. Jenkins?" she wondered out loud. Surely Bev would have wanted them here for her tryout. Then again, Mrs. Jenkins had never liked how athletic Bev was; maybe she was boycotting.

"Bev didn't tell them," Ann whispered, leaning over Mary. "She wanted to surprise them when they came out for one of Bob's games."

Mary gasped as she caught sight of James O'Grady down front.

"What?" the girls all said in unison.

"Nothing, no one—" Mary blushed and became flustered. "Oh, I mean, Ann, isn't that the boy you like?" And then she bit her tongue. Why did she have to say that? Why couldn't she just enjoy a gander of James O'Grady for herself?

"It *is* James," Maxine whispered, nudging Ann, and they all turned their heads simultaneously to see James standing behind the dugout, leaning against a chain-link fence post. He wore jeans, a black t-shirt and a blue baseball cap. His hair color and freckles hadn't changed, but his hair was shaggy and longer, sticking out from under his hat. *I wish I looked that good in freckles*, Mary thought as she gazed at him.

Ann straightened herself up, adjusting her hat, even though James was facing the other way.

In the dugout, Bev's heart had clamored its way into her throat. Her mouth was totally dry, but her hands were drenched. She was keenly aware of Conrad sitting just ten feet away. With him sat Bob, her brother, and Duncan Marsalis, the team's catcher. Bev's softball coach and Coach Riggins were talking and comparing notes. Bev was aware that James O'Grady, the boy Ann liked, was eavesdropping on the coaches' conversation from the other side of the fence.

To try to calm her nerves, Bev turned her attention from Conrad and the dugout to the pitcher's mound. She imagined herself on it, that little bump of height that made her barely taller than everyone else on the field, but when she stood on it, she felt like she was in a tower, high above all the other players, and higher even than the people in the stands. She took a deep breath, and as she exhaled, Coach Riggins called her over.

He told the boys to go warm up and said to Bev, "I'm going to have Jenkins—er, Bob—toss you a few balls to hit and then I'll have you pitch a few. I brought out Conrad Marshall because he's our best hitter. Think you can take the heat?" He smiled, thinking that by joking around with her about Conrad he was easing the pressure, but Bev's mouth went drier, if that was possible.

She licked her lips with her cottony tongue and said, "Yes, sir."

"Let's see what you can do, then, Jenkins."

Bev grabbed a helmet and, ignoring a futuristic metal-looking bat leaning against the fence, she seized the wooden bat she had brought with her. She approached the batters' box, stretching her shoulders and arms. As she crouched into position, she knew without looking exactly where Conrad was, shallow center field. He wasn't in a ready position, just standing there like he was on holiday, enjoying the weather.

Bev felt the sun on her shoulders and gleaming off her helmet. The boys' field was in better shape than the girls' softball field. This one looked perfectly trimmed and watered, a bright healthy green that looked even brighter against the clear spring sky. But the difference between the fields didn't bother her, because, after all, here she was on the boys' field! She dug the right toe of her shoe into the dirt and felt that familiar feeling: a charge from the center of the earth rippled up through her toes, her knees, her legs, her hips and right out through the tips of her fingers and to the end of the bat . . . it was connecting her to the ball before it even left the pitcher's hand.

Bob, standing on the pitcher's mound, recognized this look. He smiled. Over his shoulder, he called out to Conrad, "Yo, Marshall, you'd better play deeper."

Conrad, cocked his head and adjusted his ball cap. "Nah," he said casually. "She's just a chick with a wooden bat."

Beverly blocked him out. Bob muttered, "Have it your way," and hurled the ball toward his sister.

The ball and bat met in a thunderous crack that echoed off the stands.

"Sheesh. Swing at the first one much?" Mumbled Marsalis, who squatted empty- gloved behind home plate. As Bev rounded first, legs pumping as fast as she could, the ball streaked past Conrad's head, hitting the back fence and dribbling back towards him, as if to offer him some assistance since he clearly needed it.

From the pitcher's mound, Bob hooted for his sister and pointed at Conrad with a laugh. Conrad did not look amused.

As Coach called Beverly back from second base to hit more, she wondered at Conrad's attitude.

"Throw her a curveball," Conrad directed Bob.

"That *was* a curveball," Bob retorted.

"Hey, Marshall," Coach called out to Conrad. "Do you mind if I run my own tryout? Now why don't you try playing deep this time."

On the stands, the girls giggled and smiled, so proud of their friend. Judy was in seventh heaven: Bob was even dreamier on the field.

"Isn't he the most?" she asked no one in particular.

Conrad moved toward the outer edge of centerfield and Coach said to Bob, "Don't just lob her an easy one, Jenkins! Make her work for it!"

Bob did his best to challenge Bev, but if there was anyone he couldn't pitch to, it was her. They had played ball together since they could both walk and besides her natural talent, he was pretty sure she could read his mind. He picked a signal from Marsalis that he liked and threw his best knuckleball.

Again, the ball smashed into Bev's bat and whistled towards Conrad. Bev didn't want it to go to right or left field, she wanted it to go directly to Conrad. Well, right *past* Conrad. And it did.

"Is that a home run?" squealed Judy from the stands. The girls had stood up involuntarily. They couldn't help but cheer. Below them, James nodded happily, writing something down in a notepad. Even the coaches looked pleased.

Maxine was pretty sure she heard her cousin cuss as the ball sailed about two feet above his glove and then dropped on the other side of the fence.

After about ten more pitches, six of which were base hits, Coach wanted to see Bev's pitching arm. She warmed up, tossing a few to Duncan Marsalis. Then she indicated to Coach that she was ready.

"Batter up!" Coach called. Bev watched as Conrad told Bob that he wanted to hit first. As he approached home plate, he stared Bev down. Out of habit, she swiveled her right foot in the dirt, calling up that deep energy. She had an involuntary flash of a memory of yesterday at lunch. She had been eating with Ann and Judy and looked over to see Diane Dunkelman practically draped all over Conrad. As this image seared her brain, Bev let out a hard breath and let the ball fly.

"Whoa!" Conrad stumbled back and Coach blew his whistle. "I don't know how the girls do it in softball, but in baseball, the pitchers wait 'til the batter's up!" taunted Conrad.

With a surge of alarm, Bev realized she'd pitched the ball before Conrad was even settled into the batters' box. Her face burned.

"It's alright, Jenkins. Just take it easy and concentrate," Coach encouraged, but he was chuckling. Bev didn't know what made her madder–Coach laughing and shaking his head or the smug look pasted on Conrad's beautiful face.

She waited while, with drawn-out exaggeration, Conrad stood in the box, stepped out, held up his bat, then dropped it, looked at it with intense concentration, then decided to readjust his batting glove. Finally Coach said, "We get it, Marshall. But this ain't your show. Let her pitch to you, already!"

"Go, Bev!" Judy called from the stands. Bev watched her brother turn to look at Judy and she felt the beginnings of a smile twitch on her lips. Then it was the right moment, she could feel it: everything in the universe urged the ball out of her hand in one smooth quick motion.

"Strike!" called Marsalis, laughing.

Conrad shook his head, ever so imperceptibly, but settled back in immediately to go again.

Once more, Bev let the ball fly. It started high, and then about two feet in front of Conrad's face, it dropped and floated into the strike zone as Conrad's aluminum bat cut through empty air above it.

"Strike two!" Marsalis hollered.

"I can count, Duncan," Conrad grumbled quietly.

Once again, Bev felt a smile start to form, but she stopped herself. *Don't let him rattle your cage*, she told herself. She wasn't doing this to make Conrad look like a fool. He seemed really frosted at her. As good of an athlete as Diane Dunkelman was, she was even better at being a girl; Diane Dunkelman obviously knew that boys had their place and girls had theirs. If Bev wanted Conrad to respect her, or notice her as a girl, she surmised she needed to take notes from Diane Dunkelman. And from her own mother, who was always encouraging her to be more *ladylike*.

Attempting to shake her head clear, she wound up and without allowing herself to focus, she released the ball. It shot towards Conrad and in a blink, he was crumpled on the ground. She'd nailed his leg.

"Conrad!" she screamed, and before she could stop herself, she was rushing to him. He sat up, his head wobbling while he rubbed his ankle. She kneeled next to him. "I'm so sorry, Conrad. Are you OK?" Still not thinking, she slid her arm around him, practically cradling him. She could feel his body heat and smell his sweat. He gazed up at her and she caught her breath. A look that lasted a half a second passed between them, but it felt like it went on for an eternity. His sepia-colored eyes softened; a trace of his cute grin loomed on his lips. And then as quickly as it came, it was gone. He pushed her away.

The rest of the world suddenly rushed back, louder and more garish than before. Coach roared, "Jenkins! You're not trying out for head nurse, you're pitching! Get back on the hill!"

Trying to control her trembling body, Beverly rose. "Yes, sir." She trotted back to the mound, attempting to get a hold of herself. As the thought of Diane Dunkelman and Conrad tried to crowd her thought again, Coach told Conrad to take a base.

"I wanna hit off her, Coach. Let her pitch to me. I'm all right," Conrad said. The moment between them had passed. He was back to sneering at Bev. As she glared right back at him, she realized, *But I'm not Diane Dunkelmen. I'm me, and Coach asked me to try out for the boys' team, not her.* When Conrad was set, a rush of confidence tingled through her and the ball whizzed from her fingertips, buzzed right down the middle and she heard the catcher call, "Strike three! You're out, Marshall!"

Everyone laughed when they heard Judy whisper loudly, "Do you think she made the team?"

That night as Bev lay in bed, her mind raced over and over the details of her day. After her tryout, Coach had offered her a place on the boys' varsity team. Bob had given her a hug and Marsalis had tried to slap her hand with his fist–whatever that meant–but Conrad had stridden off in a swagger, totally ignoring her, like he had better things to do. She had played in her first game just a couple hours later and Coach let her pinch-hit in the eighth inning. She had searched the stands for her parents, but they had been nowhere to be seen. Two of her brothers, Gary and Jerry Jr., had been there, though. She wondered if Bob had told them she'd made the team. Having them and the girls there had been a great comfort.

When she was up to bat, there had been two outs and two men on. All she had wanted was to bring those runners home so Conrad would have to take notice, in front of the full stands and both teams, of the fact that she could play with the boys just as well as anyone. Only with her focus on Conrad instead of the game, she had felt totally scattered, and like a goof, she had struck out, swinging three times in a row at pitches nowhere near the strike zone. The team had won without her help, but she was heart-broken over her performance. Or lack of performance. For the rest of the game, she had tried to avoid being in Conrad's line of sight, but after the game, he had chucked her on the shoulder and said earnestly, "Good game, Jenkins."

She'd be happier if he'd given her a dirty look, or acknowledged her grody at-bat. But . . . *Good game?*

She hopped out of bed, flinging the covers back, and paced the floor with her bat in her hands. Then she reached for her school notebook. Turning the bedside lamp on, she found a clean piece of paper and ripped it out, and with a pen wrote:

~~I love~~
~~I really really like~~
~~I like~~
I <u>hate</u> Conrad Marshall!!!

She then folded the paper neatly, tucked it under her mattress, climbed back into bed with her bat and fell into a deep sleep.

11

Fancy Meeting You Here

Dear Diary,   9th of May

It's only 9 am and already I have an entry for you. This isn't a good sign for the rest of my day! To catch you up because I didn't write last night: still flipping out. Still in the future. This morning, I woke up at 8 o'clock like I do every Sunday and got dressed for church. The kids were watching television! There was food strewn all over the living room, real goopy-like. I went to Mother's bedroom to make sure she was OK; she wasn't even up and dressed for church. She was sound asleep! I reminded her about church, and all she said was, "Oh, Sweetie. You're such a good girl. You can go to church with Nana if you want, but I have an open house today." Since when is church optional, I ask you? So I went and found Nana and she acted surprised that

I wanted to go with her. We're leaving in a few minutes . . . without the kids, who will probably take advantage of this time TO READ MY DIARY. If they can read, that is. Can monsters read?

Always yours truly,

Mary Jane

PS- This afternoon, I'm thinking of sewing myself that new dress.

PPS- I saw James yesterday at Beverly's baseball tryout. I wish Ann didn't like him so much, or I'd let myself admit just how keen he is. Beverly got on the boys' baseball team. That NEVER would have happened . . . you know, BEFORE . . . .

-MJ

Dear Diary,   May 8

Today was a day I will never forget. I spent most of the day with Bob. I actually didn't spend it literally with him, but I got to watch him all day. Bev, my future sister-in-law, got to try out for the boys' baseball team--and made it!!! She was real good, too. I'm happy for her for two reasons:

1. I'm happy for her and proud of her. ♡
2. I will come see every game and get to cheer for both her and Bob. ♡

I think Bob looked at me in the stands at least twice. I don't know how to get his attention without him thinking I have cooties. The other day at lunch, I saw him sitting with Maxine's cousin and lo and behold, there came Diane Dunkelman to flirt with them all. Who does she think she is? What makes her so radioactive, anyway?

Mom is out every night with Mr. Streeter, like Daddy never even existed. I don't know how to ask about what happened to him. As you know, Diary, we girls all agreed to help each other find out what's going on here in the future. But we were all a little distracted by boys today. Even James O'Grady was at the tryout and game. Even though Ann likes him, I noticed Mary kept turning pink, straightening her skirt and sweating. It was warm out, but I wonder if she's keen on James O'Grady, too. He's pretty cute. But not as cute as You Know Who

On Cloud Nine, ♡ Judy Jenkins ♡

I still hate C.M. Even though he was 3 for 3 with a base hit, a double and a home run yesterday.

Bev

I am not black or white

I am invisible

I am not wrong or right

I am divisible

The answer is right in front of me. But all I have are questions.

M.E.M

8 May

Dear Irina,

I think I'm writing these letters into a void. I'm no closer to finding you, my old life, or the truth. But I've had a nice day thinking about something . . . or someone . . . else for a change. I watched James O'Grady at my friend Beverly's baseball tryout and game. Now if he talks to me on Monday in art class, we'll have something to say to each other. I'm exhausted. Time to pile up some Z's. I can't wait to hear back from you. Maybe a letter will arrive this week.

—Ann

Mary couldn't help but notice James O'Grady at Mass, first of all because it was James O'Grady and second of all because the church wasn't nearly as full as it had been in the past. She had tried her peony hat and gloves again, but like Conrad had when Beverly had pitched to him, she struck out. A few folks dressed a little more nicely than normal, but she was still stunned to see miniskirts, low-cut shirts, and no jackets or ties on the men. Once again, she was the fream in a flowered hat. She sat with Nana in the back and tried to concentrate on Father Steve (whom she had known by his last name–Father *Murray*–before) and his message of God's timeless love. But her eyes, thoughts and heart kept drifting to the front far right pew where James's red head bobbed up and down at all the right times; down to pray, up to listen.

During the ride on the way home with Nana, Mary stared out the car window at all the sights that had changed while a downpour coated everything with glossy rain. Bigger houses, more crowded streets, taller buildings. Everything seemed so showy–the very opposite of her–in spite of the drab gray day. Even Nana's car had excessive buttons and switches and light-up screens. At one point, Mary had been looking forward to learning how to drive, but she could never do it now. Not with this car, not in this new universe. She didn't fit in before, so how out of place was she now?

Nana sensed Mary's melancholy. "What did you think of Father Steve's sermon today?" she asked to start a conversation, as the windshield wipers thump-thumped to clear a view ahead.

"Nana, why does everyone call him Father Steve, instead of Father Murray?"

Nana smiled. "I guess to make him more 'accessible'."

"Wouldn't it be better if things were . . . like they used to be?" Mary knew she was being vague with Nana, but she had in mind the years before her father had left, and even days ago, when girls dressed decently and people knew what was expected of them.

Little did Mary know that her grandmother had the exact same thoughts; but Nana said, "Life is all about change, honey. Nothing stays the same. Except how much I love you. You can count on that." Nana reached over and gently wiggled Mary's ear. Mary allowed herself a weak smile.

Nana's silver hair reminded Mary of Mrs. Fairview at school. But Nana had Mary's rounded features and was more heavyset than Mrs. Fairview. Which was fine with Mary because it made Nana nicer to hug.

After several hours at home with all that "change" her grandmother spoke of, Mary had to escape and asked to go to the library. When Nana offered to drive her, Mary said she'd prefer to walk (hoping the library was still only about a mile away). Plus, the storm had cleared up.

She strolled leisurely at her own pace, daydreaming about the dress she wanted to make with her precious sewing machine. She thought of Father Murray's words that no matter where we are, we are loved. She wanted to ask him if it was also true that no matter *when* we are, we are loved. Maybe she should go to confession and confide in him her plight; but what would she say? "Father, forgive me for I have time traveled?"

Shaking her head to clear her thought, Mary took note of the trees lining her street, how tall and broad they were now. They provided some nice shade from the afternoon sun that came out in extreme bursts as huge skittering clouds rushed across the sky to catch up to the storm that had gone on without them. They looked sorry to have missed all the action. Mary knew the feeling. Down several blocks from her house, she cut over another block to the busier street where the library was, passing a new glittering drugstore on the corner, though it hardly resembled the Woolworth's that had been by Jenkins Hardware. This new store on the corner was in place of what had been a dusty old hobby shop that Mary had never seen anyone go into or come out of. Now, there was a steady stream of patrons who, like the clouds, moved hastily to and fro.

Past a few more storefronts, halfway to the library, was her former elementary school, set back from the street by a blacktop parking lot, newly repaved with clean yellow stripes and arrows. Though the building now had a brick front and updated windows, the structure was the same; she felt a lump in her throat as she approached. Deciding to take a slight detour, she headed to the back of the building where the playground was.

The play equipment was new, brightly-colored, gaudy plastic. The merry-go-round was gone, replaced by two long, low parallel bars. She used to love the higher bars, the monkey bars, and could hop from three bars away to the next bar. She probably did look like a little strawberry blonde monkey swaying mid-air on those. She smiled to herself at that memory and then spotted the swings.

She uncharacteristically dropped her books without a care where they landed and ran to the swings. She climbed on the middle swing, already dried from the rain by a hard-working sun, and squeezed her legs back, sprung them forward, and repeated until she was airborne. She felt the familiar burn in her palms as she grasped the metal chains with her hands, sucked the wind in through her nose as the air current pushed her up and back, down and forward. She closed her eyes and listened.

It didn't sound much different: the rush of air, birds chattering in nearby trees, distant traffic. Her hair fluttered around her face, falling out of its ponytail, and out of the chiffon scarf wrapped around it. She didn't care. Back and forth she went in a steady rhythm, so happy for this heavenly limbo she could have cried.

"Hey."

She flinched at the voice, her swinging rhythm jarred. Her eyes snapped open and as she struggled to adjust to the light, she swore she saw . . . .

"I didn't mean to scare you, sorry," said James O'Grady.

"Gee whiz! I was just . . . you didn't . . ." Mary tried to slow the swing down so she could straighten herself out.

"Don't stop for me. OK if I join you?" He cocked his head and squinted in the brightness that had just broken through a passing cloud.

"No; I mean, yes, you can . . . ." Mary could not form a sentence. James's hair flicked out in every direction, all the ends ablaze in sunlight. He looked like he was wearing a dazzling, orange, spiked halo.

James hopped on the swing next to hers and started pumping his legs as Mary had done, but it looked smooth and effortless when he did it.

"You're Mary, right?" he asked, flinging his feet out in front of him. He was wearing jeans and a white t-shirt. But never mind that . . . he knew her name!

"Mary, yes. And you're James?" she confirmed (as if her diary wasn't overrun by his name).

He nodded. "I saw you at the tryout yesterday for Beverly Jenkins."

At the mention of Bev, Mary thought of Ann. "Yes, I was there with Ann. You know Ann Branislav, don't you?" In mentioning Ann, she was doing her best to be honest; she couldn't go around trying to steal boys for herself that her friends liked.

"Ann and I have art class together."

Mary had started swinging again and now they were in sync.

"I saw you, too," Mary said. Then to be more specific–since she was nearly always on the lookout for him–she clarified, "At Bev's try out. Why were you there?"

"I was doing some writing about it," he said cryptically, then added, "I think it's pretty cool that they let a woman try out for the men's team. One of the few cool things to happen at that school, you know?"

"Why would they let her try out, do you think?" Mary wondered aloud. It was still surprising to her.

"Well, first of all, she's good. Second, it's great press. And then there's also the whole Title Nine factor."

Mary nodded, looking into the distance towards the school, which she now noticed had several trailers along the far back side, presumably for added classroom space. The main building was twenty-five yards away and she could see construction paper cut-outs, finger paintings and colorful signs in the windows. She could almost smell the paper and paste, but preferred to be here, present with James, getting a whiff of his shampoo on the breeze. She didn't know what a *title nine factor* was, but made a mental note to find out.

"It's nice that you . . . care," said Mary.

He laughed. "I kind of root for the underdog. You know, since I am one myself."

Mary's heart walloped loudly in her chest, doing double time to the rhythm of the swing. Life was crazy: just when she was nowheresville, she had found a moment of peace and James O'Grady of all people had dropped down with his halo-hair, like a ginger-haired angel straight from heaven.

She'd been watching him from afar for so long, ever since the parish Christmas party six months ago, and she had so many questions for him. But she didn't want to scare him off. She wanted to be a lady. What would her friends do? And then she remembered Ann again. It wasn't a matter of scaring him off because he wasn't hers to spook, she reminded herself.

"You seem kinda quiet," James noted. "Are you shy?"

He was absolutely dreamy! Mary fumbled. "Uh, no. I just think–a lot. Too much." Oh, terrific. Just what a boy wants: a girl who thinks too much!

"*I hear, yet say not much, yet think the more,*" James quoted. Slightly embarrassed by her expression, he said, "Sorry, I'm a geek. Shakespeare. Guess you're not the only one."

Mary laughed. "Meaning, you have the problem of thinking too much?"

"You sound shocked! Don't I seem like someone who thinks?" he teased. "I just quoted from *King Henry VI!*"

Mary's face burned. She hadn't meant to insult him.

"So, Mary, since you're someone who thinks too much, let me ask you a question. Don't you agree as a rule that people don't think enough? I mean, wouldn't it be nice if people were *more* thoughtful?"

"Yes!" Mary's hair fluttered around her face like she was in a speeding convertible. Her normally cautious demeanor was slipping away. She exclaimed, "Like parents! Parents should be more thoughtful."

"Exactly. You read my mind!"

"What did *your* parents do?" Mary felt forward in asking.

He shook his head and smiled, but it was a sad smile. After a long pause, he admitted, "They're getting divorced."

Mary dropped her feet to the ground suddenly, braking herself and the swing to an abrupt stop. "Mine, too!" she nearly yelled, and then covered her mouth. She hadn't meant to be quite so dramatic.

James stopped swinging also. "You would think it's not a big deal, right? I mean, everyone's parents are divorced. You just don't think it'll happen to you."

Everyone's parents are divorced? Her Travel to Tomorrow project was evidently way off base. Not that that was a newsflash. She blurted, "*Ann's* parents aren't divorced." She just wanted God and the universe to know that she was doing her best to be loyal to her friend.

James looked at her funny, and cocked his head in that adorable dreamy way. "Well, then I guess you and I have something in common and Ann can't be in our Divorced Parents Club."

He then reached toward her face and her heart stopped beating altogether. She froze . . . or melted . . . or some weird combination of both. "Your glasses are falling off," he said, readjusting them. She hadn't even noticed.

When she got home that night, she ran to her room and stared at herself in the mirror. She was glowing, not just red and blotchy like usual, but dewy-looking; her eyes sparkled and she could not keep her lip muscles from forming a smile. Her hair was a grody mess, thanks to the humidity, the wind, and the swinging, but she didn't care. She flung herself on her bed, lying on her back, relishing every detail of her moments with James as she stared at the ceiling and tapped the Singer sewing machine in its case next to her. She hadn't even gone to the library after he'd left the playground at sundown. She had just walked home on a cloud.

There was a knock at her door. "Can I come in?" Her mother poked her head in.

When Mary agreed, her mother closed the door behind her and sat at the foot of Mary's bed. When she saw Mary's expression, she seemed relieved.

"I've been worried about you the last few days," Mrs. Donovan said.

"I'm feeling better," Mary couldn't help beaming. "I think I need to not be so afraid of . . . change."

She could feel her glasses crooked on her face again. She didn't care.

12

What's Past is . . . Present

"I want to get together with you, honest; but I have practice with the guys now," Beverly said, changing out of her sneakers and putting on her cleats.

The girls locker room was a strange combination of muggy and slightly chilly, and Bev's voice echoed off the cement brick walls. Judy sat on a cold metal bench with peeling paint in front of Bev's locker, and Mary stood clutching her books to her chest with Ann and Maxine on either side. They were all eager to move forward to resolve their dilemma by comparing notes; and the thought of hanging out with hep friends didn't sound so bad either.

"Maybe I should stay and watch practice," Judy offered and everyone groaned. "What?" she asked innocently, but even she knew everyone knew her true motive and she laughed.

A sugary sweet voice with a hint of a southern drawl cut through from the other side of the room. "Well, well, if it isn't the star of the guys' baseball team, Miss Beverly Jenkins."

The girls turned in unison to see Diane Dunkelman in her softball uniform swinging a white school towel. Her sleek blonde hair cascaded over her shoulders. Her perfect makeup looked out of place with her athletic clothing. One hand was on her hip, and at her side, another of Bev's former teammates stood looking sheepish, like she'd been coerced against her will into Diane's sphere of evil.

"Hiya, Dunkelman," Beverly said dully, turning her attention back to her cleats. She wished Diane Dunkelman would drop dead twice.

Diane tossed one side of her hair over her shoulder. "Nice debut on Saturday, Bev. Bet your new team was real proud of you. How'd you do again? Oh, yeah. Struck out." She giggled, like it was a really funny joke. "You must be bummin' hard."

"What'd you do in Saturday's game? Oh, right. They didn't ask YOU to be on the boys' team." Everyone was startled that Maxine had spoken up. Well, she'd had a bad day and wasn't in the mood for this doll's attitude.

Diane laughed, but she didn't sound amused. "You're feisty, just like your adorable cousin."

"You stay away from my cousin!" demanded Maxine.

"And stay away from Bev's brother!" added Judy, sticking her nose in the air.

Diane laughed again, more derisively. "Chillax, girls. It's not up to me to stay away, the boys come to me. I don't know why!" She gestured at herself in fake innocence with a wave of her hand. "Maybe it's the way I dress." She said pointedly, "I mean, look at y'all! OMG, what are you, some kind of gang? You call yourselves the Fifties Chix or something?"

Mary stepped forward. "Yeah, for the fifty chicks we gave knuckle sandwiches to for messing with us!"

There was a moment where everyone in the room was trying to decide whether to laugh or take it as a real threat, but Mary held her ground. To be safe, Diane decided to retreat.

"Whatevs. Y'all are weird. Good luck, Jenkins. You're going to need it." She turned in a huff and added to her friend, "Let's go."

Her friend gave Bev an apologetic look and followed after Diane on her invisible leash. When they left, the girls burst out in cheers.

"I thought you were going to give *her* a knuckle sandwich!" giggled Ann.

Judy hugged Mary; Bev and Maxine laughed.

"I actually like the name Fifties Chix," Mary admitted and they all agreed.

"Fifties Chix forever," Judy enthused, her ponytails bobbing delightedly.

Beverly sighed. "OK, Diane Dunkelman talked me into it. How about tonight after dinner we get together?"

When the time came to head over to Judy's, Maxine couldn't get out of her house fast enough. She had done her best to do her homework, locked in her room with her quill to escape the bizarre other-world that had become her home; but there was no escaping the other-world in everything, including her homework. She'd had an anxious feeling all day after learning in history class about the Civil Rights movement of the 1960s, including a black woman named Rosa Parks who had refused to sit at the back of the bus in Montgomery, Alabama on December 1, 1955 . . . only months after Maxine made this leap to the future.

Listening to her history teacher, Mr. Steinberg, Maxine's mouth had fallen open. She imagined the uproar, not only in Alabama, but all across the country. It was the start of something huge that no one at the time could have truly fathomed: Dr. Martin Luther King, Jr. had led a black boycott of the Montgomery bus system and a year later the buses had been desegregated by order of the U.S. Supreme Court. Dr. King had been threatened, arrested, abused and attacked and his house had even been bombed, but he had remained peaceful and stayed the course.

Maxine remembered some discussion of Dr. King in her household in the past; he had been working for civil rights as a member of the executive committee of the National Association for the Advancement of Colored People in 1954. She knew now what her parents couldn't have known then: that after years of peaceful protests, rallies and marches, Dr. King would be shot and killed in 1968. Just when Maxine had felt hope kindling in her heart and pride tingling up her spine, Mr. Steinberg described that fateful day in April when Dr. King had been assassinated by a white man in Memphis, Tennessee. The injustice of it all was nearly unbearable, and the conspicuous silence on the issue in her own home was deafening. Why weren't they all still talking about Dr. King? And why weren't they actively trying to follow his lead? Had electing a black president relieved them of the fight? Was it really all over now?

Maxine had finally called her sister Melba, but she had been too busy to talk. The sound of her voice made Maxine want to weep; but she had wanted so much more, some sign that she could tell Melba what had happened to her and Melba could offer advice or somehow help.

So on her walk to Judy's that evening, Maxine felt a mixture of relief and despair. Relief at the prospect of seeing her friends, and dread over the thought of going back to 1955, which she now knew was the heart of a generation of unrest. But staying "here" was no more comforting.

Maxine walked the three quarters of a mile to Judy's in the golden light of late evening; she noticed the pre-summer days were lengthening perceptibly. She arrived several minutes after Mary, who had looked at Maxine with anxious green eyes and a nervous flush in her cheek. Maxine had a funny feeling that maybe Judy and Mary had been talking about her behind her back and her defenses shot up.

Upon seeing her, Mary didn't notice Maxine's uncharacteristic moroseness. Instead, she thought of how Maxine was such close friends with Ann and how she hoped Judy would keep her secret. Because just moments before, Judy had come right out and asked Mary if she wanted to go steady with James O'Grady. After stuttering, stumbling over her own thoughts and words, and blushing uncontrollably, Mary had finally told Judy about seeing James on the playground.

"How long have you liked him?" Judy had asked.

"Since our parish Christmas party," Mary had admitted, but hastened to add, "but Ann likes him and I won't stand in her way."

"I won't tell Ann, if that's what you're jumpy about, but I think you should tell her you like him. She doesn't own him, Mary. And besides, what if James picks you?"

Mary had adjusted her glasses. She hadn't expected Judy to take her side. She wasn't even on her own side.

Judy had twirled a blonde pigtail around her finger and murmured, "All's fair in love and war." With the word "war," she thought wistfully of her father.

"Who said anything about love? Or war?"

It was then that Maxine had knocked at the front door, leaving Mary feeling decidedly undecided. Ann soon followed, dropped off by her father, and last came Bev, freshly showered with damp hair and more out of sorts than usual.

Once again they went to Judy's room and closed the door. Though it was a warm day, and they could have been more comfortable in the open, air-conditioned living room or kitchen, they all preferred the familiarity and intimacy of Judy's room.

Mary glanced nervously at Ann; Judy watched as the shoulders of Bev's t-shirt darkened soaking up the dampness of Bev's hair; Maxine looked distant as she nibbled her pinky nail. Everyone seemed on edge, and it was obvious that their situation was nowhere near closer to being resolved.

Speaking as if in mid-conversation, Judy said, "We obviously need a plan, or a plan B. Or something. Hasn't *any*one found out *any*thing that we were supposed to?"

They each were finding out lots of things . . . but as far as they could tell, nothing that could help answer their questions. Besides, there were lots of distractions of late . . .

"This clearly has to do with our Travel to Tomorrow project. I wish there was a way we could read our assignments again." Mary longed to get her hands on those papers, feeling there must be a clue there. But they'd handed them in to Miss Boggs and she hadn't been seen since. "What are we supposed to be *learning*?" Mary wondered out loud.

Suddenly Maxine snapped. "This isn't an assignment, Mary. It's life, real life. Who knows why things are the way they are! Do we think we're going to change anything? This whole thing is bummersville and I'm sick of it!"

Everyone was forced into a stunned silence by Maxine's sharp tone. It was Judy who spoke up a few moments later. "Maxine's right. We agreed on Friday we'd get to the bottom of this, and a whole weekend was wasted."

"Wasted?" Bev interjected. "I beg your pardon, but my weekend wasn't wasted. I tried out and got on the *boys' varsity baseball team*! Do you think that would have happened in 1955?"

Mary was still stinging from embarrassment from Maxine's outburst. Mary hadn't meant to upset anyone, and she was fairly certain none of this was her fault. In fact, despite her few heavenly hours with James, she was doing more researching and clue-gathering than anyone, having spent the afternoon at the library. While feeling scolded by Maxine, she also understood Maxine's frustration. She, like Mary, was probably discovering just how much the world had changed in fifty-five years without their getting a say in it at all.

Maxine heaved a sigh and said, "I'm sorry I yelled, Mary."

"It's OK," Mary responded. "We're all out of sorts. And I think if we did re-read our travel to tomorrow projects, we'd see just how far off about everything we were." To that, they all agreed.

The atmosphere was already heavy, but Mary recalled what she had discovered earlier. She had wished she had the guts to mention it sooner, but the subject of James had come up and she was distracted. So now she took a deep breath to calm her nerves and said, "Judy, I have something to tell you."

Again, all the sound and air seemed to be sucked right out of Judy's room and everyone sat motionless. Only Judy knew what Mary was going to tell her. "It's about my Dad, isn't it?"

Mary nodded and Judy said, "I already know."

"How? Did you talk with your mom?" Ann asked, hoping that one of them had taken the bold step of having a conversation with one of their parents.

"No. Follow me." Judy left the bedroom with the girls in tow. She went to the kitchen table, no longer a Formica and metal table top, but a thick piece of glass balanced on a huge cube of stone. Judy pointed to a flat metal box and they all gathered around her and stared. "This told me." She wasn't sure she had wanted to reveal to the girls just yet what she had discovered, but the moment had presented itself.

"What do you mean, *it told you*?" Maxine whispered.

By way of explanation, Judy lifted the lid of the box and a screen on the top inside lit up. The bottom was like a flat type-writer.

"We have one of these, too!" Ann said.

"It's a *computer*," Judy said. What had been a shorthand class at school was now a computer science class. She had been completely lost, spending the time doodling Bob's name on her notebook, but just today she had started to pay attention and thought it might be useful. She was right.

"A computer?" Mary thought the notion was ridiculous. Judy was very proud of her stereo and the fact that her household had the unheard-of quantity of two TVs, but the notion of owning a computer was utterly ridiculous. Computers were complex machinery that took up entire rooms! There were only a couple hundred in the whole world, so for Ann to chime in about having one too was off the wall.

Beverly had seen several such machines in her own house; it seemed like everyone had one, including even her mom. It was one of the many things on Bev's list to find out about. Right after getting on the boys' team and figuring out Conrad Marshall, that is.

"Watch this," Judy demonstrated. "I saw my mom with it last night, and I started playing around with it later. She pushed this blue button . . . then this box appeared . . . and now I can type in anything I want and it will find it for me. See?"

A search engine popped up on the screen and the girls all gasped involuntarily as the name of Judy's father and a picture of him appeared.

"His name is Robert, too . . . " Bev noticed in a solemn whisper. Judy nodded as her eyes filled with tears. She clicked another button and the screen filled with information:

Robert Samuel White
Specialty: Navy SEAL
BUD/S Class: 184
SEAL Service: 10 years
Rank: Petty Officer First Class
Age: 32
Assigned: Naval Special Warfare Development Group
Died: March 1, 2005
Operation: Enduring Freedom (Afghanistan)
Details: White was killed in combat during a clandestine insertion . . .

Mary couldn't bring herself to read the rest of the "details," but her eye caught the words *'open in the event of my death'* letter further on in the text. "Have you read the letter?" Mary asked Judy.

Judy shook her head no; after finding this information about her dad on the computer, she had looked through all her mother's drawers and closets, but could find no evidence of her dad. Not the letter he'd written to his wife and daughter, or even one of the twelve medals or five ribbons he had earned.

"They must be in a very special place," Ann speculated hopefully.

Maxine, feeling brave, asked, "That was Afghanistan. But how did he die in Korea–in the 1950s, do you know?"

"Well, Mom wasn't so secretive then. We had pictures of him up and she told me he was in a special Naval unit that went in towards the beginning of the conflict, in 1950. But . . . no matter how you look at it, then or now, he's gone." Tears coursed down her cheeks.

The girls all shared one aching heart at that moment, wishing they could be of comfort. Mary felt terrible; she was so frosted at her dad, but at least she still had one. And now he was back in her life, like a second chance she hadn't dared ask for.

Surrounded by her friends, Judy started to feel a glimmer of something promising, but it was shattered when the door from the kitchen to the garage opened and her mom walked in balancing two bags of takeout food. "Hi, girls!" she said brightly.

Judy quickly slapped the top of the computer closed, but it only attracted her mom's attention and she said laughingly, "What are you looking at?"

The girls closed in around Judy and greeted Bitsy in an attempt to distract her. Bitsy was only temporarily sidetracked by the funny clothes the group was wearing, but she wasn't fooled by their chipper welcomes; she put the bags on the kitchen counter and came towards Judy.

"Hiya," Judy said, standing up to give her mom a kiss.

"Alright, now I know you're up to something. Let me see it." She reached over her daughter and opened the computer lid. A look of shock come over her pretty face, and she said without taking her eyes off the screen, "Girls, do you mind if I have some time alone with Judy?"

"Yes, ma'am," "Bye, Judy," and other farewells were muttered as the girls gathered their things quickly to leave. Mary gave one last look at Judy, whose blue eyes shone with a borderline-frenzied pleading. Mary gave a weak apologetic wave and closed the door behind her.

The four girls stood on Judy's front porch.

"I feel terrible. Should we have left her like that?" Maxine asked.

"What could we do?" Ann said.

"Do you think Mrs. White is real frosted?" Bev wondered wistfully, tugging at her still-damp pony tail and tucking the loose strands behind her ear.

"Poor Judy," Mary murmured.

The sun had just set, casting an apricot glow all along Judy's street. With the lighting so soft and hazy, the street looked practically peaceful and nostalgic; until a shiny low-riding silver car with black-tinted windows rolled by, rattling everything within a ten mile radius with a horrific, bass-grinding sound that was presumably considered music. The contrast made Mary giggle.

Story of my life, she thought. The other girls must have thought the same thing because they all laughed, too.

"My ride's not coming for another half hour," Maxine noted. "I think I'll walk." They started to walk together; it would only be for a block before Maxine would head in the opposite direction from everyone else.

They agreed to check on Judy the next day at school and try to get together again as soon as possible. After saying their goodbyes, Maxine turned left and crossed the street. She immediately got lost in her own thoughts and didn't notice Bev until she caught up to Maxine and touched her shoulder.

Maxine jumped.

"Sorry," Bev said, waving bye to the other girls. "I just thought . . . you might like some company."

"Don't you live half a mile in the other direction?"

"Well, yeah, but I could use the exercise. You know, with baseball and all that."

Maxine was actually glad to have the company.

They walked in silence a few moments, taking in their surroundings. Many of the small ranch houses that they had been familiar with had either been remodeled or torn down and replaced with oversized two story houses with three-car garages and small green patches for front yards.

Maxine opened the way for the conversation Bev wanted to have by asking, "How was baseball practice?"

Though she had been hoping to talk about this, Bev still felt unprepared, so she stuttered along. "It was–hard. Not great. I mean, I did OK . . . ."

"Are the guys giving you a hard time?"

Bev nodded. More like *The Guy.*

"Guess it's adjustment for everyone, not just you," mused Maxine.

Bev nodded again, then said, "Can I ask you a question?"

"Sure. Fire away."

"Well, I'm curious about your cousin."

"Conrad?"

"Yeah, Conrad," Bev said, as if just remembering his name. "He seems . . . . " Bev struggled to conceal her feelings for Conrad, but desperately needed advice on how to get his attention.

"What?" Maxine found herself ready to defend Conrad.

Bev started. "Well . . . I can't seem to do anything right in his eyes, and I feel like . . . if I can get his approval, the rest of the team might come along." It was her best attempt to not come right out and say that she really didn't care what anyone other than Conrad thought.

Maxine thought about it for a minute. She didn't know much about this new Conrad, but she knew what her mother did when her parents weren't getting along. "My mama always asks my daddy to fix something when they fight, and the next thing you know, everything is swell."

"Maxine! You're the most! Of *course.*" Bev's ponytail bounced, and a spring in her step that had been missing reasserted itself. She smiled.

"What about your brother, Bob?" Maxine asked. "Is at least one of your teammates nice to you?"

"Oh, sure, Bob and the team are boss," Bev said absently, absorbed in her thoughts.

"But you just said the team–" Maxine could tell Bev wasn't listening, so she said, "Never mind," and wondered about Beverly Jenkins.

13

Only You

Dear Diary,   May 10th

After school, I went to the library and found out what happened to Judy's father. I mean, this time around. See, I had to stay after class to talk to Mrs. Fairview on Friday. I didn't mention this before because it's HUMILIATING, but I just burst out in a class with a wrong answer. Well, maybe it wouldn't have been wrong, you know, <u>before</u>, but it was wrong on Friday. I felt like a clod. I found out there isn't a Soviet Union anymore! The cold war is over! We're at war with Afghanistan now, I think. Anyway, that's what it looked like when I went to the library and looked up Judy's dad's record. It's a matter of public interest, so I wasn't snooping too much (I think Nancy Drew would have been proud.) When I was going to tell Judy, she already knew after all. She found it on a COMPUTER at her own house! This story just gets kookier. Anyway, seeing her cry over her daddy, who was a real hero, made me think about my dad. Maybe he's not so bad after all. At least he's alive.

    I didn't see James today. The bright side is that it gives me more time to find out about the title 9 factor he mentioned. It feels like forever since yesterday. But it's been forever since last week for sure . . . or maybe only fifty-five years.

    Always yours truly,
    Mary Jane
PS- Tomorrow I make my new dress DESPITE home ec (which is no help at all now when it comes to sewing)!

Is life bound to be just a series of heartbreak and loss, just when things start to look up? I am trapped between a dark history and the bright future without a map.
" Maybe that's what life is. . . a wink of the eye and winking stars." -Jack Kerouac
M.E.M

Dear Diary,   May 10

May my sweet Daddy, Petty Officer First Class
Robert S. White, rest in peace. I found out today that
he was killed in Afghanistan. I looked on a map. It's
even further away than Korea! I wonder what his last
thoughts were—I wonder if he thought of me and Mom.
I hope he knows I love him. I hope he knows he'll always
be my Daddy. I found out all about him today after
school on the computer. When Mom found me, she made
the girls go home right away. I thought she was hopping
mad, but she wasn't. She cried. She said she misses him.
She said she didn't put out his pictures or medals or
ribbons because every time I saw them I cried and it
broke her heart. I don't remember doing that. I feel
crushed. I hope he doesn't know that we hid his
pictures and tried to put him away. It's my fault. I
cried and told Mom I missed him and I wanted to see
his pictures, his letters, his medals, and everything. She
went out to the garage and came back with a big box.
She looked so happy as she took everything out one by
one and showed me. She still loves him, I can tell.
And I still love my Robert.
Good night, Diary. I think I will sleep much better
tonight!
Sweet dreams,
♡ Judy "Jenkins" ♡

Baseball practice was horrible. I couldn't do anything right. Conrad laughed at me. Laughed right in my face. Not like my brothers . . . I can take their teasing. This was different. It got under my skin and the more mad I got, the worse I did. I wished he would drop dead twice! But then I talked to Maxine and now I have an idea.

Bev

Dear Irina,   10 May
I got up the nerve to talk to James today. I
haven't told anyone else yet. In art class, we were
assigned to do a report on our favorite artist. . .
and we both chose Jackson Pollock!! Mrs. Leach
said we couldn't both have the same artist, so he
chose Andy Warhol instead. He said, "I'm
impressed you like Jackson Pollock; I'd have
thought you'd be a Georgia O'Keefe kind of girl."
Well, the idea that he'd think of me at all just
puts me on cloud nine! He has this red hair that
he doesn't wear in a duck tail or anything, it's just
kind of long and soft. And his eyes are sweet and
gentle . . . probably just like his soul. James
O'Grady is a dreamboat. It was close to being a
perfect day . . . until we all went to Judy's house
and found out how her father had been killed in
the war. My heart broke for her. And I felt my
throat get tight thinking of you and hoping you
haven't met some similar fate. I know I just need
to ask my parents. Why haven't they said anything
about you or your father? I think I've discovered
a way to find out . . . But until then, I will not
give up on you. Or on me.
◦–Ann

Mary sat in third period "home sciences" class and stifled a yawn. This was nothing like the home ec class she was used to; before, she had learned to prepare a roast, bake a pie, stuff a turkey, ruche the front of a dress, darn socks, make an apron with matching kitchen curtains, and of course sew her own clothes. In this new class, she was balancing a checkbook and going over healthy, low-calorie menu options. She was daydreaming and staring out the window (thinking of you-know-who) when Mrs. Doss caught her attention.

"I know you've been looking forward to this all year, and next week the babies are coming. Our end-of-the-year project will be a crash course on parenting."

Mary snapped to as a few kids cheered and a few others groaned. Mary glanced at the girl next to her, Katie Shipman, and whispered, "*Babies?*"

"The computerized babies," Katie said enthusiastically. She was one of the kids who had cheered. "Mrs. Doss told us about them at the beginning of the semester, remember? They eat, cry, sleep, and everything!"

"And . . . *everything?*" gulped Mary.

Katie giggled. "Yep! And, it's like, half our grade. Which is good for me because I totally failed that household budget chart thing we did."

Mrs. Doss interrupted them. "Ladies, I know you're excited, but you don't want to miss this information. These babies are very intricate and expensive pieces of machinery, so before you learn how to be parents, you're going to have to learn a few basic technical things for your projects, so listen up."

There was a strange rushing in Mary's ears and she missed what else Mrs. Doss said; she was busy trying not to faint.

In fifth period, there was no time to try to catch the others up on her home ec project. They wouldn't believe it! But her priority was, like the rest of theirs, to make sure Judy was doing alright after the news of her dad. Judy had barely had time to explain that her mom had shown her everything of her dad's and there were pictures of him back on the walls when the bell rang.

Before facing forward at the start of class, Bev noticed Conrad in the back of the room; but feeling relieved by Judy's update and hopeful about her plan, she wasn't concerned about Conrad today. After class, she absentmindedly accepted Judy's invitation to come over after practice.

After school, she dressed eagerly for practice and jogged out to the field. When she was doing infield practice, she wasn't even disturbed by Conrad calling out, "You throw like a girl!" She just laughed along with the guys.

At batting practice, she made her move.

"Hiya, Marshall," she said casually as he stood watching Bob take a ball.

Conrad seemed surprised, but he said, "Uh, hey."

"I hate to bother you. But you're the best hitter on the team, and it was really humiliating how I struck out the other night at the game. I was wondering if you could give me a few pointers?" She tilted her head and tucked her hair behind her ears, like she'd seen Diane Dunkelman do when she talked to boys.

He looked like he wanted to come back with some wisecrack, but thought better of it after she had complimented him.

"Um, yeah. OK," he said awkwardly. "I noticed when you get nervous, you close up your stance."

"Oh, I didn't realize," Bev said, her heart racing. *Be cool,* she told herself. "Can you show me?"

"Why don't you ask Bob?" Conrad said, taking his eyes off her and gesturing to her brother.

She was afraid he would ask that, but she was ready with a quick response. She lowered her voice. "Bob can't hit as well as you."

A smirk played on his mouth then. "I can show you a few pointers after practice."

Acting surprised, Bev said, "Gee whiz, Conrad. Thanks!"

The boys in line behind Bev snickered, but she didn't care. Conrad went ahead in line and went up to bat, smoothly hitting nearly every pitch with his bolstered ego. The rest of practice, Bev couldn't help noticing that his snide comments toward her had gone by the wayside and he even encouraged her occasionally. Now she just had to manage a one-on-one tutorial with him without her knees turning to jelly.

Bev stretched in the dugout while the rest of the team headed to the locker room after practice.

"You coming?" her brother Bob called out.

"I have to stay after for a bit, then I'm going to Judy's. Can you pick me up there later?"

"Being your chauffeur doesn't pay enough, *Jenkins,*" he said shaking his head good-naturedly.

"Thanks, *Jenkins,*" she called out sweetly as Bob waved and jogged away.

Conrad lingered behind. He cleared his throat. "So . . . what do you wanna know?"

Bev felt the nerves set in. She tried to tell herself this was a coaching session and nothing more. But her heart knew better and couldn't be fooled.

At eight o'clock, Judy stopped wondering if Bev was going to show up and decided to take a shower and wash her hair. Her mom was working late again, so she'd been on her own for dinner. But Judy didn't mind; she'd had the afternoon to herself to use the computer to find out about the Jenkins' hardware store and couldn't wait to show Bev what she'd discovered.

She put the Platters on her record player in her room and sang and danced to "Only You" as she towel dried her hair. The doorbell rang and she gathered her robe, tying it in front, tossing the damp towel on her bed.

"Better late than never, I guess!" she said as she swung the front door open.

Only it wasn't Bev on her front doorstep. It was Bob, Bev's brother Bob, *Robert Jenkins*, in the flesh! And Judy in her robe with wet hair. She gaped at him like a deer in headlights, finally coughing out a shocked, "Bob!"

"Judy, right? I'm here to pick up Bev. I honked out front, but I guess you guys didn't hear me . . . with the music . . . " He paused, listening to the Platters playing in the other room, and a questioning look crossed his face.

"Oh, I know," Judy said, trying desperately to smooth her dripping, unruly hair as she spoke. "My mom thinks rock and roll is just noise. I can turn it down . . . ?"

"That's OK, just send Bev out," Bob said, turning to go wait in the car.

"Wait!" Judy stalled. She ran to her room, yanking the needle from the record (hoping she hadn't, but ultimately not caring if she had scratched it). Her eyes darted around the room, but there was nothing she could put on her head to cover her hair. "Coming!" She called out to Bob as she threw on a summer dress, flinging her robe across the room.

As she debated dabbing a little perfume behind her ears, she heard Bob call, "Bev?"

He was going to think she was a psycho! Scrapping the perfume, she rushed back out. "Bev is . . . actually, not here yet."

"Oh," Bob said, confused.

"But I'm expecting her any minute," Judy said hastily, hoping to delay his exit. "Can I get you something to drink? Ice water or pop? We have soda pop, in the kitchen," she clarified.

"No, thanks," he said, and then took a few strides forward, his attention on the pictures of Judy's dad she and her mom had just set out on a sideboard in the living room. "Hey, is this your dad?"

Judy nodded proudly.

"I didn't realize he was in the service," Bob said, intrigued.

"He was a Navy SEAL."

"Was? I'm so sorry," Bob looked up, meeting Judy's gaze. "When–?"

"In Afghanistan," Judy stumbled over the timing. ". . . A few years ago. Mom and I moved here last year."

"Is that a bronze star?" Bob asked, gesturing toward the medal. Again Judy nodded. "Your dad's a real hero."

Judy beamed with pride, forgetting about her sopping hair. Bob Jenkins was in her house and admiring her dad's service. And just think, if he'd come two days ago, the pictures and medals would have been packed away!

"You seem real interested in the military," Judy noted.

"Oh, yeah. I'm thinking about enlisting after high school," said Bob, continuing to look over the pictures and awards of Petty Officer White.

"You can't!" Judy burst out.

Bob laughed. "What?"

"You're such a swell athlete. I mean, I watched you when Bev played . . . I just thought you'd want to play in college."

"That's what everyone keeps telling me. But sometimes the more everyone tells you something, the more you wanna do the opposite, you know?"

Yes, Judy did know.

"Look how cute you are." Bob winked. Judy blushed, and then saw that he was pointing to a picture of her daddy laughing with her as an exuberant flax-haired toddler giggling on his shoulder. Judy had seen a similar picture years ago; only that picture had been from before her daddy had sailed into the South Pacific, not the Middle East.

Bob glanced at his watch. "Maybe I should go try to find Bev. She stayed late after practice. Mom would kill me if I lost my sister. I don't have a spare!"

"I could be your spare," Judy joked in a lame attempt to flirt. Unfortunately, she had just offered to be his sister, which was not at all how she wanted him to think of her.

"It's a deal." Bob smiled. "Although, you look nothing like Bev. I don't think Mom would be fooled."

When Bob left, Judy dreamily watched him drive away and then ran back to her room to finish crooning "Only You" in his honor. The cats hid from her under her bed, but she wasn't offended. 1955, or fifty-five years later, she didn't care. Life was grand!

"I'm home!" Her mother called from the kitchen. Judy skipped in to give her a welcome home kiss. Bitsy laughed, hanging up her keys. "You're practically glowing," she said to Judy.

Judy grinned, tilting her head this way and that and shrugging her shoulders theatrically.

"Well, that makes two of us," sighed Bitsy. "I think I am really falling for Roger."

Her boss, Mr. Streeter?

And like the screech of the needle dragging across a record bringing her favorite song to an abrupt ending, Judy's euphoria was dashed.

14

Duck and Cover

Maxine could tell Ann wasn't really listening to her; while Ann had one eye on Maxine, she had the other eye on James across the room. Maxine had decided to do her art report on Frida Kahlo and was discussing it with Ann. She had so much more to talk to Ann about than a school report, but since Ann wasn't listening anyway, Maxine just stopped talking.

In such a short amount of time, all of Maxine's friends had seemed to resign themselves to this future world; some of them even appeared to be enjoying it. It just made Maxine feel that much more alone. All they were interested in were boys and dating. What about serious issues, like human rights, civil rights, and world peace?

Maxine made a decision. "Can you excuse me a minute?" she asked Ann.

Maxine crossed the art room and went right to James O'Grady, who was sketching a detailed picture of a Campbell's soup can for his Andy Warhol project. When Ann saw Maxine approach him, her mouth fell open. Ann's mind raced . . . what would her friend possibly want with James? In a split second of panic, Ann wondered if Maxine would say something about Ann's crush on him. But Maxine would never . . . .

Ann couldn't hear their conversation. It was very hushed and neither Maxine nor James looked over at her or gestured in her direction. Ann tried to act casual as she went back to flipping through her Jackson Pollock book, straining to eavesdrop on their conversation.

A few moments later, Maxine came back to where Ann sat tortured. Maxine seemed brighter, happier, somehow.

"What did you say?" Ann asked in a quiet whisper.

"Well, uh, actually, I'm not allowed to tell you. But I promise it wasn't about you."

Ann looked horror-stricken. Maxine placed a reassuring hand on Ann's shoulder, "I promise it wasn't about you. It was about the art project. But he did say he digs your hat."

Ann's eyes lit up and she touched her gondolier hat. "Really? Gee whiz!" She glanced at James with a smile and went back to her book with a flush in her cheeks.

For the first time in days, maybe weeks, Maxine felt a faint glimmer of optimism.

She wished she could keep the girls in orbit about her news, but the whole point was to keep it a secret. When she had found the booklet and started reading it, she had felt her heart leap. She had salivated over the delicious words chosen and how the articles were written. It was a collection of poems, prose, fiction and editorials. It was student work, but the authors had made-up names to remain anonymous. She had read a beautifully written article called "The Boys Make the Big Time." It was a commentary on Beverly Jenkins's being allowed on the boys' varsity baseball team. But it was written from the point of view that it was the boys' team that was making progress by having Bev come on board; not that it was Bev who had made a big step up. The by-line was Jackson O. Maxine knew it had to be written by James; Jackson in reference to his favorite artist and O for O'Grady.

When she had initially approached him in art class about the underground rag, *The Invisible Truth*, he denied knowing what she was talking about. But when she had said she had just read and enjoyed a little piece called "The Boys Make the Big Time," he had blushed ever so slightly. He hadn't admitted to it being his, but he hadn't denied it either.

"I just want to show you some things I've written," she had said.

He had nodded. "OK," he had said, and quickly changed the subject. "Ann looks like she should be in a painting."

"I know. Great hat, don't you think?"

He had agreed. "Bring me whatever you want to see; but this is not a public club, and the school administration is especially interested in who's writing for the paper. *No one* can know, so keep it on the down low."

"My lips are sealed," Maxine had promised.

Now sitting at lunch, she enjoyed her secret while Judy and Ann prattled on happily. A million times, Judy had gone over the conversation she'd had with Bob when he had come by to pick up Bev at her house last night; and Ann told Judy that she and James O'Grady had the same favorite artist. Well, if they weren't going to listen to Maxine, she'd just have to find an audience who would appreciate what she had to say.

On her way to fifth period, where she would see Conrad for the first time since practice last night, Bev thought of the sheet of paper under her mattress. Last night she had pulled it out, unfolded it and added a strike-through to the last line. It now said:

As she slid into her desk, she noticed that Conrad wasn't in the room yet. She smiled (as she had been doing uncontrollably all day); this way she could watch him walk in and see if he looked at her first. But as she arranged the books on her desk in anticipation, a siren suddenly blared from the classroom doorway. She whipped around and looked at Mary, Judy, and Maxine, who were already seated.

An air raid siren! There was no way of knowing if it was only a drill.

Terror shot through each one of the girls and in perfect unison, they dropped to their knees and went under their respective desks, in exemplary duck and cover formation as they had been taught and as they had practiced dutifully many times over the last several years.

As kids were filing in, they groaned at the siren, and then as they caught sight of Bev, Mary, Judy and Maxine under their desks, laughter raced around the room like wildfire.

"OK, that's enough!" Mrs. Fairview had to loudly address the guffawing over the continuing blare of the alarm. "It's a fire drill, so line up outside near the front school sign for roll call. Let's go!" She directed the students on her way to the help the girls out from under their desks.

Embarrassed, they crawled out quickly and clumsily.

"We're sorry," Mary stuttered. "We weren't trying to be disrespectful . . ."

They all muttered awkward apologies. Mrs. Fairview wasn't sure what to say. It had been fifty-five years since the last air raid drill at this school.

"It's alright. I'm sure you just mistook it for a tornado siren. Let's just get outside quickly for the count." She walked briskly to the door with the girls, her arm around a trembling Mary's shoulders. She reassured them quietly, "It's alright." Mary didn't notice that Mrs. Fairview's gold watch caught on her sweater. Mrs. Fairview quickly disentangled herself, covering her watch back up.

The girls followed Mrs. Fairview outside, feeling more conspicuous than ever and exceedingly foolish. Bev was grateful that by some twist of fate, Conrad hadn't been in the classroom to see it. She should have known it wasn't an air raid siren; a few years back her Pops had built a bomb shelter in their basement. It was very expensive and constructed with the best materials to resist an a-bomb attack; but it was kept a secret so that the neighbors wouldn't crowd their doorstep when they were bombed. It was just big enough for her family and some food.

But the other day, Bev had noticed that the basement was now just a storage area. She didn't know if she should take it to mean the bomb threat had lessened, or if her parents were simply unprepared.

After school, before heading to practice, Bev stood with Mary, Judy, Maxine and Ann in the school hallway. As kids filed past them, in the buzz of a day that didn't quite get back on track since the fire drill, some of them snickered at the girls.

Diane Dunkelmen, flanked by two of Bev's former softball teammates, passed by for the sole purpose of saying loudly, "Check it, it's the Duck and Cover Girls!"

The other students milling about in the hallway burst into laughter and Diane was pleased with the spotlight. She winked and smiled at Bev as she tossed that silky hair behind her shoulder with an arrogant flick of her head.

"I think I prefer being called the Fifties Chix," muttered Bev.

"No question," agreed Ann.

Mary added, "On the bright side, at least we don't have to worry about being bombed by the Soviets."

They said their goodbyes and parted ways: Ann to pick up her brother, Mary to make herself a new dress, Maxine to go do some writing, Bev to go to practice and Judy to loiter near the baseball field in hopes of catching a glimpse of Bob.

Bev had a great practice putting the advice Conrad gave her to good use, with only one little nuisance: Conrad himself wasn't at practice to see her. No wonder she did so well–he wasn't around to rattle her cage.

Coach even said, "Great practice, Jenkins," and reminded her of the team's upcoming games the next day and Saturday. After thanking Coach, Bev called Bob, who was on his way to the boys' locker room, over. Even though he'd be driving her home in a few minutes, she couldn't wait to know a moment longer.

"Where's Conrad Marshall?" she asked.

"Word on the street is, he's the tool that pulled the fire alarm today. He got hauled in to the principal's office after school. I heard Coach say Marshall might be suspended. Which stinks for us; we have two games we need him for to get into the district playoffs." Bob shook his head in disappointment and then looked up toward the bleachers and noticed Judy. "I think your bestie Judy's waiting for you." He waved at her and she waved back. "Still want a lift?"

"Sure," Bev said. Then she glanced at Judy. "She might need a ride, too."

"No prob, dude. See ya in a few, then." Bob punched Bev playfully on the shoulder before he left for the locker room. "But hurry up, it looks like rain!" He pointed to the sky.

Bev gave Judy a thumbs up, who returned it with a big grateful smile. *At least something good might still come of this day,* Bev thought.

But on the way home, as Bev sat in the back seat, she resented having too much time to herself to think about Conrad: *what could he have been thinking to pull that prank?* Judy and Bob chatted in the front of the car; he pelted Judy with questions about her dad's naval service. *Judy must be in seventh heaven,* Bev sighed to herself as she watched it start to rain outside, *talking to Bob about her dad.* Sometimes other people's lives seemed so simple . . . .

Maxine sat at her desk and stretched her hand. She hadn't looked up for hours and now noticed that her bright yellow room had darkened significantly. Storm clouds swirled outside her window and fat raindrops started to plunge from the dark gray heavens above. Maxine had come straight home from school to her room, closed the door, opened her notebook to start writing and hadn't stopped. She had used her great-grandmother's quill and a bottle of ink. The middle finger on her right hand was throbbing and stained with ink, and her paper had little blotches and blobs on it, but she didn't care.

As she took a deep breath now, she felt like she was waking up from a satisfying and restful nap. She glanced around her room with fresh eyes. Daddy and Uncle TJ had painted the room she had shared with Melba the color of sunshine when her sister had gone off to college; it was to keep Maxine cheered up. For the most part, it worked; it was difficult to be too depressed or lonely when the walls surrounding you were the color of giant buttercup petals. The two twin beds, desk, chair and dresser were a matched set with dark glossy wood and rounded lines. Because she was feeling refreshed now, it was easy to see all that she had to be grateful for. Her parents did everything they could for her so she would never feel poor or like a second-class citizen. Just as her thoughts began to wonder why her room and clothes were the only things that had remained the same in the last week or so, she saw both her parents' cars (before Mama didn't have a car, or even a driver's license!) pull in, followed by Uncle TJ's car.

Her parents came in through the garage and kitchen, while Uncle TJ dashed from the curb to the front door. She watched as Conrad slowly pulled himself from the car and sauntered inside, as if it weren't raining buckets by now. Maxine closed her notebook to go see what the fuss was about. It was early for Daddy to be home.

Maxine found them in the kitchen, all staring at Conrad and silent.

"What's going on?" Maxine asked cautiously.

Only Conrad looked at her defiantly. The adults continued to glare at him.

"Would you like to tell your cousin what's going on?" Maxine's mama said.

"It's not a big deal—" Conrad started.

"Not a big deal?" roared his dad, Uncle TJ.

"No, it's been blown out of proportion!"

Maxine sought clarification. "What has?"

"Go on," Daddy encouraged his nephew. Evidently the adults wanted to hear Conrad himself say it.

"I pulled the fire alarm today," Conrad admitted. "It was a *joke!*"

"You caused the air raid siren?" Maxine said, putting her hands on her hips. Now the adults' eyes all shifted to Maxine. "I mean, the fire alarm . . . ." She felt her face go warm.

"It was a joke," Conrad reiterated.

"Is it a joke that you're being suspended?" demanded Uncle TJ.

"Yeah, it is a joke. The school should suspend people that are actually hurting people or doing something wrong!" retorted Conrad. Maxine was stunned to hear him talk to his father this way. No one in her family addressed adults disrespectfully.

"Do we need to remind you of this?" Mrs. Marshall waved a piece of paper in the air. "This is the bill for the fire department having to come on out to your school today. This is the bill the school wants you to pay. How you gonna pay for it, son? You don't have any money. Your daddy doesn't have any extra money."

Nobody dared suggest that Conrad's mama pay the bill; she had taken Conrad's four sisters and little brother and moved to Louisiana and was hounding Uncle TJ for money all the time, even though three of her girls weren't Uncle TJ's. When she had gone, Conrad had wanted to stay with his dad, aunt, uncle and cousins, Melba and Maxine.

Conrad shrugged, looking down. At first he looked repentant, but then he slowly looked up and met his aunt's angry eyes. With a gleam of pure rebellion, he said, "Put it on my tab."

"That did not just come out of your mouth, Conrad Terrence Marshall! You take it back right now!" Thunder rumbled as the words shook the room. Only it wasn't Maxine's mama's voice . . . it was Maxine's. Everyone gaped at her in shock. "Do you have any idea what your family, and the brothers and sisters who've gone before you, have sacrificed so that you can go to a white school, play baseball, go to college if you want to? You have it so easy, and you are just throwing it away! Do you think Rosa Parks sat in front of the bus so that you could pull a fire alarm? Do you think those nine brave kids from Little Rock integrated Central High so you could walk around school hollering, swearing and acting like you own the place? Do you think Dr. King was killed so you could be an ignorant hoodlum? Do you think having a black President gives you permission to slack off?" Maxine was yelling now, partly out of passion, partly to be heard over the storm raging outside.

No one responded.

"*Do you?*" Maxine screeched, demanding an answer. She had just spent the afternoon writing about all those that had gone before her. It had finally dawned on her that things were not hopeless, it was just the opposite. But this generation seemed so self-absorbed; there was no sense of community, no burning desire for progress, as if they had arrived and there was no more work to do. The result of that was a serious lack of respect for history. She saw it everywhere she looked and it was crushing her heart.

Finally, Conrad said, "No."

The adults remained in stunned silence.

"Conrad, you're better than that. I know you," Maxine said. "Maybe it's not right that they suspended you for that prank, but the Conrad I know wouldn't have pulled it in the first place."

With a subdued tone, Uncle TJ said, "Gloria and John, we will pay you back—"

Conrad interrupted his dad again. But his tone was different. "No, *I* will pay you back. I'm sorry." He looked down at his feet, remorseful, and glanced up at Maxine. He'd never seen or heard her like this.

When Uncle TJ and Conrad left, Maxine's parents still stood rooted to the floor, gazing at their youngest daughter. Their incredulity had melted into admiration. At last, her daddy came and hugged her close, and then her mama joined them. Maxine started to cry and wondered if she'd ever stop.

15

Sincerely

Ann held on to her hat with one hand and balanced her books with the other hand. The wind was picking up and the air smelled like damp earth; a storm was on its way. She soaked up the color of the steel gray sky and wondered if she would mix that color with burnt sienna and ultramarine, or with cadmium orange and cerulean blue?

"You know you don't have to walk me every day. I'm eleven," her brother Alex said. He strolled next to her on their way home after school. It was the first day in a week that he had forgotten his tiny little portable music player with the little wired bobbles that fit inside his ears. They didn't talk much on their way home when he was listening to music on his little machine, and Ann was never sure if she should be relieved or feel alienated because of it. Today she definitely felt relieved that he *didn't* have it.

"I know I don't *have* to walk you. But I actually don't mind it," Ann said.

"I kinda like it, too," Alex admitted. Ann glanced at her brother out of the corner of her eye. She wondered how he made his way in this brash new world; he seemed fragile in every way, physically, emotionally . . . even his hair was delicate. Silky thin wisps of light brown hair framed his sweet, boyish face. As a painting, he was beautiful, but as a junior high schooler, he got picked on a lot. It didn't help that his interests lay in reading, science experiments and building strange contraptions. He didn't play sports or hang out with other kids. She missed the sight of the *yarmulke* he always used to wear, even though she was sure it probably made him even more of a target. His best friend, Franco, was just as quiet and mysterious.

"Are you going to the school dance?" Alex asked, heaving his overstuffed backpack from one shoulder to another.

"What school dance?"

"Your school's having a dance on Saturday," Alex said.

"How is it that you know about *my* school dance?" Ann laughed. She was about to give up on this hat; the brim might as well have been a sail as it fluttered erratically in the breeze. It nearly lifted her right off the sidewalk.

Alex shrugged. "Franco's sister is going."

"Right. And who is Franco's sister?"

"*Diane*," Alex said with a trace of impatience. Didn't his own sister pay attention to anything? She was so dreamy and absentminded all the time.

Ann stopped short and a book slipped out of her stack. *"Diane Dunkelman? Franco is Diane Dunkelman's little brother?"*

"Duh," Alex said.

It took a moment for Ann to absorb this. She just hadn't come across Diane Dunkelman much before she'd befriended Beverly and hadn't made the connection between her and her brother's little friend. Then Ann had a thought and groaned, as Alex picked up her book and carried it for her. They started walking again.

"Who's she going with?" Ann asked. She felt like a fream for asking her ankle-biter brother for vital stats.

"It's all over facebook. That baseball guy, Bob."

Ann jerked to a stop again. *"Bob Jenkins??"*

"Yeah. Why?"

"No reason. I just didn't know . . . and I'm friends with his sister," Ann said, keeping her concern for Judy to herself. She wondered about James O'Grady. Was he going to the dance? Had he invited somebody? And what in the world was a "face book?"

Ann's thoughts were interrupted by her brother. "Can I ask you something, Anna?" He always referred to her by her full name.

"Of course." She was enjoying the idea of having an actual conversation with her little brother since . . . *before.*

"What's with the getup? You know, dressing kinda funny and acting kinda weird. Franco's sister said everyone's starting to call you and your friends the Fifties Chix. I told Franco if he ever called you a name again, I'd beat him up." He added with a grumble, "His sister's mean."

That was a lot of information to take in. "You threatened to beat up your best friend?"

"Well, yeah. You're my *sister.* Besides, Franco couldn't hurt a fly."

Ann wanted to add, *Well, neither could you,* but didn't want to ruin the moment.

"So why do you dress like that and stuff?" Alex squinted up at her. She was still taller than him, but it wouldn't be long before he shot up. Their father was six foot four.

"This is who I am, Alex," Ann said. "It's not a getup; it's just . . . me."

"Oh. OK," Alex said with simple acceptance. Ann wanted to sweep him up in a big grateful hug, but knew that he would probably not consider that a nice treat.

Before she lost her nerve, she said, "Alex? Do you know how I can get in touch with our cousin, Irina?"

Now he stopped suddenly in his tracks. He seemed worried. "What about her emails? Have they stopped coming?"

"Her . . . what?"

"Her *emails*?" He squinted up at her again.

"I have old letters . . . " Ann stammered, "but nothing, uh, recent . . . "

"Have you been able to get online? Maybe they took the servers in Belgrade offline again."

Ann was worried the conversation could come to this: she had no idea what he was talking about. But she'd started the conversation, so the only thing she could do now was ask, "Can you help me?"

From: Irina Brajer
Sent: May 04 10:37 PM
To: Anna Branislav
Subject: The guy

So tell me more about this wonderful guy, my sweet cousin. I need a distraction from life in Belgrade. Father is living in the past. He

treats me like a child and thinks only of Serbia's "glory days." I ask him, "When was that, Father?" because I don't remember any glory days. It's all fighting and violence and no peace. I miss Mother. Distract me and tell me about this James! You can tell I need it!
Sincerely,
Irina

From: Irina Brajer
Sent: May 05 8:31 PM
To: Anna Branislav
Subject: re: The guy

I'm surprised I haven't heard from you. Are you being secretive about James? ;) Father says hello and thank you to Auntie Katrina for the groceries and supplies. They were delivered to our flat; who knows how much went missing, but we did get meat and light bulbs.
Sincerely,
Irina

From: Irina Brajer
Sent: May 06 11:16 PM
To: Anna Branislav
Subject: r u ok?

I hope I haven't offended you. It has never taken you more than a day to write me back. Is everything OK? Please let me know.
Sincerely,
Irina

From: Irina Brajer

Sent: May 08 2:30 PM
To: Anna Branislav
Subject: r u ok?

Are you on a date with James? Haha . . . I hope that's where you are.

I met an American soldier in Belgrade. He is in the Air Force, stationed in Bosnia. Can you imagine me telling father I've fallen for an American soldier? He blames the US for the NATO attacks on Belgrade. Does the rest of the world even know about this or care? Should I care, or should I just run off to America with my soldier? He is from Kansas City. Is that near you?

I'm starting to worry about you . . . Please write soon.

Your cousin,

Irina

Ann sat stunned in front of the bright computer screen. After helping her open an email account she didn't know she had (and didn't know how to open), Alex gave his big sister a weak pat on the shoulder and left her alone, even though she was on his computer. As she started to breathe a sigh of relief, a sob rushed out with her exhale. Ann was so thankful; Irina was alive and well and wondering if *Ann* was alright. She re-read the emails over and over as the sky continued to cry with her.

Bev doubted she had gotten even a wink of sleep; she had tossed and turned all night thinking of Conrad and how she could get him to play in Thursday's game. By the time she and

Bob had dropped off Judy and arrived home, Bob had gotten word that Conrad had in fact been suspended and would miss the next day's game.

Bev hadn't eaten anything for dinner, but no one noticed because the evening suppers that had once anchored the Jenkins family were no more. Her mother was rarely home, Pops always worked late, and the boys were heading in a million different directions. Now if you were hungry, you ate standing in the kitchen on your way to your next activity, or while catching part of a game on TV. The other night Bob had asked her, "Where are you going to stand?" while they ate dinner at the counter. Bev found herself washing dishes every time she passed through the kitchen; there was an ever-growing pile in the sink. She was astonished her mother would allow it, but she watched her add to the pile once on her way out the door.

Ann had explained what she had discovered about Pops's business: it had been sold years ago and then torn down to make room for the new hardware store monstrosity. They had hired Mr. Jenkins immediately to manage the store since he knew the business so well. But he now worked longer hours for less money and less satisfaction.

Bev recalled the old family dinners at six o'clock on the nose. Pops left the hardware store at 5:30, arrived home at 5:45 to put on his slippers and enjoy his pipe before dinner, and then they all gathered around the dining room table for roast beef or pork chops (which they only had on Mrs. B's day off for some reason). Everyone who had sports practice–which was everyone except Gary–was clean and showered.

Conversation was lively; Mrs. Jenkins required each family member to bring a topic to discuss, although sports was limited to only teams the boys where on, or the whole discussion would degrade to a Cardinals-Cubs sound-off.

Once, when it was Bev's turn to introduce a subject, she had asked, "Do you think it's more fun to be a boy or a girl?"

Her brothers had burst out laughing, and her Pops had smiled broadly at her.

"A boy, of course!" Bob had responded for all the males. "You get to play sports and do whatever you want!"

That's what Bev had been thinking and found herself agreeing silently with her brother.

"Oh, Robert," Mrs. Jenkins had demurred, shaking her head gently. "It's much more fun to be a lady." She winked at Bev. "You get to dress up, have a good man fall in love with you, and keep a lovely home. What could be better?"

At the time, Bev had been able to think of a lot of things that could be better.

But last night as she had cast herself around, getting tangled in her sheets while sleep eluded her, she wondered why she couldn't have all of those things? . . . Or just one of them?

In hopes that music might soothe her into slumber, she put on her McGuire Sisters record and turned it down low. Her last memory before falling asleep were the lyrics, *Sincerely, oh you know how I love you, I'll do anything for you, please say you'll be mine; Please say you'll be mine. . . .*

"Coach?" Bev tapped the door of his office. She was glad to have found him. The first bell for school hadn't rung yet and she needed to talk to him right away.

"Jenkins," he said, turning around from a filing cabinet. "Come on in."

"I won't take too much of your time," she said, tucking her hair behind her ears. Her pony never stayed smooth and perky, and more and more lately, she felt sloppy.

"What can I do for you?" he asked, turning back to the filing cabinet, looking for something distractedly.

"I was just wondering . . . " Bev chose her words carefully. "What the team could do to get Conrad Marshall to play."

"Unfortunately, the team can't do anything. Conrad lost that privilege when he pulled that ridiculous stunt."

"But we need him!" she said more strongly than she had intended. "I mean, maybe it would help if the principal knew what a good team player he is. He helps us all be better . . . he helped me with my batting stance . . . ."

Now Coach turned to her with a quirky smile on his face. "Jenkins, believe me, I can appreciate how much the team needs Marshall for a win. But fact is, we're probably going to get rained out today anyway." He gestured to the window, where a steady rain had been falling since the previous afternoon. "If so, we'll have to squeeze a double-header in before the school dance on Saturday, and we'll need to be practiced up."

"Right," she agreed. "OK, well, thanks."

He'd already gone back to the filing cabinet. As Bev turned to go, she wondered about the school dance he had mentioned. Distracted, she didn't notice Conrad until she ran smack-dab into him, practically kissing his neck.

16

See You Later, Alligator

On Thursday, Maxine waited nervously for a free moment in art class, and then raced over to James O'Grady.

"Here's the book you wanted to borrow," she said loudly, shoving at him an art book she had checked out at the school library just for this purpose. Maxine thought of Judy then, coveting Judy's more polished acting skills.

James, slightly confused, said, "Ah . . . thanks?"

Maxine opened the cover slightly to reveal an envelope tucked inside.

"Oh," James acknowledged. "That was fast."

She smiled nervously and said, "You're welcome," and scurried back to her seat next to Ann. Surprisingly, Ann seemed to not notice. She was subdued today, distant, but not in her usual dreamy way.

"Everything cool?" Maxine asked.

Ann shrugged. The few charmed moments of being thrilled by the future was beginning to lose its luster.

"I know," Maxine said, without Ann having to try to explain.

The five of them were back at Judy's house after school. Since Bev's game had been postponed, they took the opportunity to get together again, calling an "emergency meeting" in light of the school dance none of them knew about; there were no posters in school advertising a sock hop, and no dance committee that they knew of to plan or decorate.

Outside, the rain continued to fall, ignoring the already saturated ground. Worms on every sidewalk did the freestyle to the other side of the puddle, and leaves drooped like sad green faces slick with tears. Maybe it was the dreary weather, but they were all starting to feel moody.

To cheer themselves up, they had hoped to make a double batch of Mamie's Million Dollar Fudge, but not one of the ingredients could be found in Bitsy's kitchen. Instead, they used a box of brownie mix they'd discovered and followed the directions to make a chocolaty-gooey batter. As they had thrown together the few ingredients, Mary explained to them what she had discovered in her research and why she thought it was that Bev was able to try out and play for the boys' team.

"It's a law called 'Title Nine' and it says that in public schools, girls must have the same opportunities as boys in sports."

The girls marveled; their situation was neither good nor bad, but the extremes of both. Bev was a case in point: while she was thrilled to play baseball with the guys, she missed her "old" family life, especially her parents.

"Have you told her yet?" Mary whispered to Ann.

Ann shook her head "no."

"Told who *what*?" Judy said on her way back into the kitchen.

During the explanation of Title IX, Judy had excused herself to get a chocolate stain off of her white cotton blouse and heard the whispering on her way back in. She didn't want to miss a thing.

"Told who what?" she repeated.

Ann swallowed hard. "Well, we called this meeting because of the dance, right?"

"Oh, I know all about the dance," Judy said. Looks passed between Maxine, Ann and Mary.

"But did you know Bob is going to the dance?" Ann asked.

As Judy's eyes lit up, Maxine quickly added, "With someone?"

As instantly as she'd brightened, Judy slumped. "Who?" she said dully.

"Diane Dunkelman," Mary shared the tragic news as gently as she could.

"*Diane Dunkelman*?" It was Bev who screeched.

"We thought *you* knew," Ann said. "You live with Bob."

"No, it's out of nowheresville," Bev said. "I hadn't the foggiest. *Her*, of all people!"

Judy, who had done her best to not indulge in the chocolate for the sake of her impending Hollywood career, now grabbed a spoon and started slurping batter with abandon.

"This is all wrong!" she said. "Not the brownies, Mary," she clarified, catching Mary's worried glance at the box. "*This* . . . the future."

"I'm not sure we can call it the future," Maxine said. "I mean, we're living it. We're here now, aren't we? It's the *present*."

"So is there a 1955 going on somewhere without us?" Mary wondered.

Ann shivered. It all seemed so spooky when they spoke of it directly.

"Well, whatever you call it, it's not right. Mom puts out all of Dad's pictures again and she's still way gone on her boss, Mr. Streeter. That's not appropriate, is it?" Judy turned to Mary. Certainly Mary's sense of propriety would back her up on this.

"What's 'appropriate' anymore? The kids–" referring to her sisters and brother– "have no respect for adults, no bedtime, dress however they want, watch television round the clock. Everyone's getting divorced–"

"Certainly not *everyone*?" Ann asked.

Mary reddened. "I meant . . . it's just a figure of speech."

"We know your parents are, but is there something else you're not telling us? Who else?" Maxine prodded, having sensed something in Mary's voice.

Mary paused before she said, "Well, there's . . . James O'Grady's parents."

"Oh," Ann sighed sympathetically. Then, "How did you know that?"

Mary's heart raced. "He goes to my church."

"And he told her," Judy piped up.

Mary glared at Judy.

"When did you talk to James O'Grady?" Ann asked, not aware that they knew each other.

Mary's tongue stuck to the roof of her mouth. But she couldn't blame the brownie batter.

"Sunday," Judy volunteered.

So much for promising not to tell! Mary seethed silently at Judy.

Ann, along with Bev and Maxine, looked at Mary questioningly.

Finally, Mary conceded, "I saw James at the school playground on Sunday afternoon when I was out for a walk and we talked a bit."

A hopeful glow emerged immediately in Ann's porcelain cheeks. "Did you happen to ask him about me?"

Mary nodded slowly, "I mentioned you several times." This was a nightmare. Whenever she thought to take up Nana's offers to learn to drive, this is what she imagined would happen; the car would go careening out of control and Mary would start pulling, pushing or grabbing at buttons and switches and accidentally make the car go even faster; she wouldn't be able to avoid hitting things on—or off—the road and wrecking Nana's car. Someone was bound to get hurt with her behind the wheel.

"Why are you acting so–" but right as Ann was asking, before she even finished her question, she understood.

"What?" Judy said, licking her spoon distractedly while Mary's and Ann's eyes were locked.

"You like him!" Ann accused.

"Oh, I knew *that*," Judy said, mostly to herself.

"I'm so sorry!" gushed Mary.

Ann said, "Well, why didn't you just tell me? How long have you liked him?"

"Since . . . Christmas," Mary admitted, ducking her head apologetically.

That's not even as long as I've liked– Bev started to think, but stopped herself. Just in case anyone in the room could read minds, especially Judy who would spill the beans to the whole world. Bev didn't know whom she felt worse for, Ann or Mary.

"It's not a crime," Maxine put in, trying to defend Mary.

"I didn't say it was a *crime*," Ann huffed. "I just thought that we were friends. I didn't know she'd try to steal him away from me, right out from under my nose!"

"It's not like that at all, I promise," Mary said with a pleading tone.

"Then why didn't you just tell me that you like him and that you saw him the other day? Why the big deal? And how come *she* knows?" Ann pointed at Judy.

Mary couldn't think straight. She just wanted this to all go away. She'd even stop liking James if she thought it could help.

"Because I'm her friend!" Judy responded indignantly.

"So I'm not your friend?" Ann turned back to Mary, who wished Judy would just shut her trap. She wasn't helping!

"I don't think she was trying to hurt you," Maxine attempted to mediate.

"Why are you taking their side?" Ann turned on Maxine.

Bev could see this was getting out of hand. She felt as uncomfortable as Mary looked. "There aren't any sides, Ann," Bev said. "Mary probably just didn't tell you because she didn't want this to happen."

Mary said, "She's right! I only told Judy because she figured it out."

"What do you mean, you 'only told me because'? Are you saying I can't keep a secret?" Judy huffed.

"I don't think anyone has to say that; you just made it fairly obvious," Maxine said.

"I don't like being accused of being a bad friend!" shrieked Judy.

All of a sudden, they were all yelling and interrupting each other. It was reminiscent of the slumber party they'd had what felt like so long ago, only this time Mrs. White wasn't around to break up the brawl. Finally, Bev whistled a piercing peal. "That's enough! We're all on edge because of our situation. We can't turn against each other; we're a *team*–"

"You know what, Bev? *Everything* isn't a *game*," Judy said bitingly. "I don't think I'm in the mood for guests anymore." She folded her arms across her chest, deliberately closing herself off from all of them.

"Well, I don't think I'm in the mood to be here," Ann grumbled.

"Just wait." Mary made a weak attempt at keeping them all together for even a moment longer. If she could only think of something to say to bail out this sinking ship. But they'd been torpedoed–by a boy–and they were going down fast. "What about the dance?"

"Forget the dance, Mary," Judy hissed. "Just split. All of you."

One by one, Maxine, Mary, Bev and Ann grabbed their books, raincoats and umbrellas. Mary didn't even stop at the door to pull her rubber boot covers over her loafers. Nobody said a word to each other until Judy slammed the door behind them.

When they had all left, Judy scooped up every bit of the remaining batter and threw it in the trash with an angry flourish. She couldn't stand the idea of Bob and Diane Dunkelman. And now her friends had turned on her. She was totally alone.

Once ejected to the wet outdoors, the four girls walked separately, even though they were headed in the same direction.

Bev caught up with Maxine to walk with her, but Maxine said with a sigh, "Not now, Bev."

Fine, Beverly thought. *I don't need them anyway.*

Which is exactly what each of the others was thinking.

17

A Stitch in Time

Maxine came home to the sound of the vacuum cleaner. Conrad was in the hall outside her room with the Hoover. When he saw her, he turned it off and gave a shy wave.

"What are you doing? I mean, besides Hoovering my house?" she said, shaking the rain off.

"Well, I also mopped the kitchen, cleaned out the rain gutters and weeded the garden. I told you all I'd pay you back," Conrad said. "Besides, I ain't got–" he saw her eyes narrow "–I *don't have* anything better to do. No school today."

"You weeded in this weather?"

"Kinda why I had to mop the kitchen floor and now I'm vacuuming."

"Oh, well. Way to go." She hung up her raincoat on the coat tree in the living room.

"So, where were you?" Conrad made conversation as he unplugged the cord and began to wind it into a coil.

She was surprised he wasn't frosted at her, after she'd hollered at him yesterday. "I was with my friends." She almost had to cough out the word "friends." Were they anymore?

"Buncha white girls you hang with?" asked Conrad.

For lack of a better response, Maxine nodded and plopped onto the sofa in the house that didn't feel like hers.

"Beverly Jenkins one of them?" he asked.

She looked at him and nodded again, wondering if Bev had taken her advice about requesting his help and if it had worked. She hadn't even asked.

Conrad shook his head, smiling, and turned his attention from cleaning. "She's alright. Did you know your girl went and talked to the coach to try to get me to play even though I'm suspended?"

"No, I didn't know that."

"Yeah, she's cool."

She thought shamefully of how she'd spurned Bev when Bev had wanted to walk with her earlier, and how she had yelled at her cousin while Bev stood up for him.

"Did you thank her?" Maxine asked.

Conrad snorted. "No!" he shook his head again, as if thanking Bev for having his back was the craziest thing he'd heard all day. And then he wondered if he should rethink that . . . .

Mary banged the front door behind her as she dashed past the twins watching TV in the living room. From the kitchen, Nana called, "Mary, is that you?"

Mary ignored her and stormed to her room, slamming that door, too. She was soaked from the rain and her face was streaked with tears.

Nana gently knocked on her door. "Are you alright, sweetie?"

"No," Mary said. "Go away." She wasn't going to worry about being disrespectful to Nana; the kids spoke to her a lot worse as a matter of course.

"I just wanted to remind you–"

"I said *go away!*" Mary cried. She heard the creaks of the floorboards in the hallway that indicated Nana was walking away. If it was possible, Mary now felt worse. It wasn't Nana's fault; but neither could she have one more awkward conversation with Nana, where Nana's concern for Mary was barely hidden. She didn't want to talk about her clothes any more, or hear how sometimes kids go through "phases," but it's OK because everyone has to "find" herself. Well, Mary wasn't lost. She knew exactly who and what she was; it was everybody else who had gone goofy.

She peeled off her wet clothes and hung them carefully to dry. After wringing out her hair, she put on the coziest PJs she could find and went to her desk. Her books were piled on the floor and in their place was her prized possession: her black shiny Singer Featherweight sewing machine.

Two days ago she had started on a beautiful light blue summer dress. She'd had the Simplicity pattern and the soft, satiny cotton fabric for a few months, but she didn't want to start on it until she was sure she wouldn't mess it up. The dress had cap sleeves with crisp white cuffs, a white peter pan collar and a row of five self-covered buttons down the front of the fitted bodice. At the waist, there was a narrow belt and buckle, only Mary had made a three and a half inch white fabric rose to use in place of the buckle. The skirt was nice and full and would fall just below her knees.

She'd started with the hard parts, the bodice and the sleeves, so she could save the easy part—the long straight seams of the skirt—for last. She arranged the pieces on her bed, gently unfolding the swatches of blue skirting that she had pinned together last night. The fabric felt like smooth tropical waters pouring over her hands, cool and refreshing, but she was careful not to snag her skin on the pins. She felt a pang of sadness as she realized how perfect the dress would have been for the dance.

Arranging herself at her desk, she turned the switch of the sewing machine on, lifted the foot to place the fabric, turned the wheel for the needle and thread to catch, and dropped the foot back down with a satisfying light thump. As was her habit, she ran her right index finger over the sparkling gold Singer decal on the machine's engine cover before she pressed the petal lightly with her right foot. This was as close as she wanted to get to driving.

The machine sprang to life, humming while it pulled the fabric smoothly along, the gentle chunk-chunk-chunk of the wheel encouraging the needle to pull the delicate thread in and out; the rhythm soothed Mary and she found the place where her heart thrummed with excitement at the thought of the completed dress. Her fingers moved deftly, coaxing the pale sapphire-colored material along in its journey. She was reveling in the fact that she had filled the bobbin last night, so she didn't have to stop to "refuel" the thread; she could just sew.

She had sewn two sets of two panels, and was now attaching one side with a seam. She had a very wide flowing semi-circle, and then one more seam and she'd have a full skirt. Besides hemming it, she only had to attach the skirt to the waist. She noticed that the storm had finally broken, and as quickly as it had come, it had dissipated; or more likely exhausted itself into nothingness. The sun now danced happily through her pink lace curtains, making ripples on the blue fabric as if it were the peaceful sea and she were having a picnic at the beach alongside it.

Lost in her own pleasant world, having prohibited thoughts about anything or any*one* else, Mary jumped when there was a knock at her door. She knew that at least it had to be an adult; the kids would have just run in unannounced and uninvited.

"Mary?"

"Come in," she said, surprised to hear a male voice.

Her dad pushed the door open cautiously as Mary stopped sewing and turned around in her chair. Twice in less than a week! Mary found this new dad a curious creature.

"Your Nana thought it would be OK if I came up. I hope you don't mind . . . hey, whatcha working on?" he said, stepping into the room. He closed the door behind him, looking at the dress parts she had laid out.

She hopped from her seat and made a place for him to sit on her bed while she held up the top of the dress. "I'm making a summer dress," she said.

He made a low whistle. "Impressive, girl. You're quite the seamstress!"

Why was he acting so courteous and kind? Why couldn't he just go away and leave her alone? He looked kind of sad sitting there. Which didn't grieve Mary so much as annoy her. She preferred her adults to have their act together.

He ran his fingers through his thinning auburn hair. "Your Nana said you seemed pretty upset. Is everything alright?" He said it in a way that made her think he really hoped she would be alright, just so they wouldn't have to have an intimate conversation. But she had been so careful with Ann's feelings, trying to deny her own and where had it gotten her?

"Everything is not alright."

"Oh. Can I help?"

Throwing caution to the wind, Mary asked, "Why did you leave us?"

He took a big deep labored breath. That was evidently just the kind of answer he was hoping to avoid having to give. "You need to understand that things with adults are complicated. It has nothing to do with you or how I feel about you."

"I'm not a child, you know. How complicated can it be? You didn't love us, so you left. But you keep hanging around." Mary felt a boldness in speaking to him and she realized the boldness came from not caring at all what he thought about what she was saying. At least maybe she'd get some answers, even if it made him angry. And maybe she'd even have some insight to share with James . . . .

"Mary," he said turning to face her. His nervousness seemed to vanish as he said the following words with great conviction. "I didn't leave because I don't love you or your mom. I love you *all*. But we weren't happy together; we got married too young and I needed to find myself."

There's that "finding yourself" thing again! How ridiculous! How hard was it to understand who he was? He was a husband and a father. It didn't take jets. Mary was silent.

"Does that make sense?" he asked when she didn't respond.

Not wishing to continue the conversation, she said, "Sure."

He seemed relieved. Before he stood up, he clapped the top of his legs. "I came to take you and the kids to dinner. You ready?"

"I wish I could, but I need to finish this dress. There's a school dance this weekend."

He kissed the top of her head. "I understand, kiddo. I'll catch you next time." As he approached her bedroom door, he paused and turned back to her. "Are we good?"

"Peachy."

Dear Diary,   12th of May

I don't know what to start with first. Ann is furious with me. But I'm furious with Judy. See, Judy told her that I like James O'Grady. Somehow everyone else is frosted too, that is, Maxine and Bev. (We found out there's a school dance this weekend and we were going to go together, since none of us have dates. Beverly's brother is going with that obnoxious girl, Diane Dunkelman.) I don't know what to think. I didn't do anything wrong liking James. Ann thinks I was trying to steal him. First of all, he would never choose me over her. She should know that . . . she's looked in a mirror, hasn't she? And second of all, I'm not that kind of girl. So maybe I'm not so happy with her that she doesn't know that and doesn't trust me.

This all makes my other news seem like a real drag: I finished the dress. It is beautiful. It's the most dreamy thing I've ever made or put on. It's the color of the sky in June. I'm putting a piece of the fabric between these pages.

Dad came by to take me to dinner. I didn't go. I looked back in my diary for the night he left. Besides the fact that I was 10 and barely keeping a diary, I wrote nothing about it. I just skipped right over that night. I remember looking out the front window at him in his felt gray hat and overcoat, carrying two suitcases to his Buick. I wondered how everything he needed could fit into two suitcases? I wished we all could fit into his suitcases . . . but then he wouldn't be leaving us, would he? Nana came the next day and moved in. No one talked about it. It was like she was coming anyway for a vacation and just stayed. Why does she want to be here and he doesn't?

I was awful to Nana. I love her so much. I do want her here. I will have to make her a new apron or something.

Yours truly,

Mary Jane

PS- I miss the girls already.

Dear "Jackson O,"
Here is the writing project I did for your
paper, The Invisible Truth. Dr. Martin Luther
King, Jr. said "a riot is at bottom the language
of the unheard." I feel a riot welling up in
me . . . I feel unheard. But I realized that the
reason I am unheard is because I am not
speaking up. So here I am . . . speaking up.
Thank you
Signed,
"Miss Thurgood"

May 12
Dear Diary,
Bob Jenkins is going to the dance with Diane
Dunkelman (Oh, there's a school dance this weekend.)
I could just die. And the girls hate me. I can't keep
my mouth shut!! I told everyone that Mary likes
James. She will never forgive me and I don't blame
her.
Judy.

I'm so glad I have brothers and not sisters. Girls are infuriating! I wish I had been playing baseball today instead of over at Judy's house finding out that my foolish brother Bob is going to the school dance with bad news Diane Dunkelman and getting bawled out by the girls for stuff I had nothing to do with. Doubleheader on Saturday against the Panthers. (Piece of cake compared to hanging out with a bunch of girls!) I am pitching the second game!! We have to win both to go to Districts. If Conrad Marshall plays, we'll win.

Bev

Dear Irina,   12 May
I got your emails!! But I hope you don't mind if this is
how I write you back. I have not forgotten you.
Yugoslavia . . . or Serbia as you now call it, is a mess.
But things are a mess here, too. One of my best friends
Mary likes James and has been seeing him behind my
back! You're right . . . I know what you are saying, she
must not be one of my best friends! But honestly, it's just
not like her. I can't understand how she would do something like this. Our other friend, Judy, told everyone about
Mary liking James. I didn't even hear it from Mary
herself! Judy was just upset, so I shouldn't blame her.
Mary even apologized for liking him. You can't help who
you like, can you? That's not why I wanted her to
apologize. I guess I just wanted someone to apologize
because this is just so hard. I want someone to make it
better. I thought it could be James. Or at least my friends.
Tell me more about the American soldier that you met!
(Whatever you do, don't tell your friends that you like him
. . . he will come between you and you'll end up hating him
and your friends!)
I miss you, Irina.
—Ann
PS - I just read the last line I wrote. Now
I understand why Mary didn't tell me . . . .

Ann stared at the blank canvas while she gripped the brush in her hands. She'd never finished the painting for the Travel to Tomorrow project, and in fact, hadn't even started it. There was nothing more intimidating than an empty canvas. Was there?

With a shiny glob of lamp black, she made the first stroke, and then another. The drama of the day dwindled in the presence of brush, paint, canvas. Crimson, lemon yellow, cobalt blue; her brush flitted across the palette, licking up colors and blending them right on the canvas. Her room filled with the odor of mineral spirits and linseed oil.

Her thoughts faded into the background, losing their harsh edges, just as her brush strokes smoothed into one another until it seemed that large portions of the image had been applied by one big multi-colored brush with a single bold flick of her wrist. Setting in the details absorbed her whole attention. Lights and darks played against each other harmoniously. She felt like she was on a balance beam, carefully treading between protecting the areas that were coming to fruition nicely and the areas that needed more work.

Time, that sneaky foe that had messed up her life, no longer had a say when the brush was in her hand. It was not a factor in this self-portrait and she felt liberated.

By the time her mother had called out goodnight, Ann looked at the canvas as a whole for the first time since starting. A colorful glimmer of a girl who looked a lot like herself was staring back at her with a knowing smile.

18

Friday the 13th

Judy was filled with dread at the prospect of facing her day alone. She would be in school with one boy who didn't know that she existed, four girls who hated her and the rest of the school who thought she was a fream. The fact that it was Friday the 13th didn't help! She put on a black dress to show that she was in mourning and taking the date seriously (although the perky white polka dots speckling her dress toned down quite a bit of the gravity she was going for, as did the pink bows in her hair). She appreciated the fact that her cats Desi and Dragnet had been sticking close to her, sensing her melancholy, but now she was even more sad that she couldn't bring them to school with her. Maybe she shouldn't even go to school today. But then again, she didn't want to miss anything . . . .

Beverly was up with the dawn; since there had been no practice the day before, she made up for it by running three miles before school. As much as she loved sports, she was not a fan of running, unless it was on the field and toward a ball, a goal, or a base. She wished she could skip Friday and go straight to Saturday to the doubleheader.

In the car on the way to school with Gary and Bob, Bev couldn't help but ask Bob about Diane Dunkelman.

"I heard who you're taking to the dance," Bev said. Gary was in the back seat finishing a "paper" (which was not on paper at all, but on one of those portable computers). Bob sat next to her, driving the car; Bev's eyes stung and she couldn't figure out why until she realized it had to be his overdose of aftershave. Her nose wasn't too thrilled about it, either. This was not a good sign; he was trying way too hard.

"Did you see that on facebook or is it getting around school?" Bob asked with a trace of pride.

"Ann's little brother heard it from Diane's little brother." Bev made it sound as unexciting and unglamorous as possible.

"Oh. Which one's Ann?"

"The one who wears the hats," Gary volunteered from the back seat.

"Right," Bob said.

"So why *Diane Dunkelman* of all people?" Bev had to know.

"Have you *seen* Diane Dunkelman?" Bob laughed.

"I've *heard* Diane Dunkelman open her big mouth," Bev said. Gary snickered.

Bev added, "And I've seen Diane Dunkelman try to play softball. Not pretty."

Bob laughed again. "I'm not interested in girls I can play sports with!"

"I'm a girl, remember?"

"Yeah, but you're my sister," Bob clarified.

They pulled into the school parking lot then and the conversation was over; at least outwardly. But Bev keep hearing the echo of Bob's words *I'm not interested in girls I can play sports with* and thought of Conrad. Maybe he felt the same way. Her stomach did a few uncomfortable flip flops, and now she had to face her day feeling a little queasy on top of all the other drama she didn't ask for.

Maxine walked to school with her palms shaking and a little sweaty. No matter how many times she wiped them on her jeans, she could not make them stay dry. She wondered if James had read her essay and she wondered what it would be like to see Ann in art class and the rest of the girls in social studies … or as they were now calling it, current events. She had the familiar feeling of being too conspicuous; for the last two years, every day when she walked to school, she'd needed to be hyper-aware of her surroundings and be sure not to attract any unnecessary attention as she walked through white neighborhoods to get to her school. She'd gone to an all-black elementary school near her house, but her parents had felt that she wasn't getting the education that she should, that separate did not mean equal, and they switched her to a white junior high and high school. She was getting an education alright, but probably not the kind they had bargained for.

She decided to think of all the things that she had to be thankful for as she walked; at the top of the list was the fact that Dr. King had done the hardest part. Look at the doors he had opened! And he would never know. She touched the gold cross that still hung faithfully around her neck and then thought of

Bev for some reason. She was thankful that Bev had stood up for Conrad.

Ann was stunned to discover that yesterday had been *Yom Ha'atzmaut*, the national independence day of Israel commemorating the declaration of the state of Israel in 1948 and the end of the British Mandate of Palestine. Ann's mother had always prepared a special meal before sundown, lit twelve candles (one for each tribe of Israel), and then said a prayer that her brother, Ann's Uncle David, would leave Belgrade (along with his daughter Irina) for Israel or the States. But Uncle David insisted he could never leave the land that was soaked with the blood of those he loved: his wife, parents and brothers.

This time the whole day had gone not only unobserved, but unmentioned. Ann should have had some warning last Saturday when they did not walk to synagogue and her mother drove around town in the car doing errands and working. There had never before been a Sabbath–Saturday–when Ann's family drove the car, used electricity or worked. Bit by bit, everything sacred in Ann's former life was shriveling into obscurity. With a fleeting thought, she wondered how bad it would be if she used *Yom Ha'atzmaut* as an excuse to miss school Friday. But of course she couldn't. Using it for selfish and cowardly reasons was worse than not observing it all.

She would just have to brace herself for what was certain to be an unbearable day.

Mary slipped the dress on carefully over her head, smoothing it over the stiff, puffy crinoline petticoat she wore at her waist, and buttoned the front. It fit perfectly. She had wanted to debut the dress Sunday at church with white gloves (since she wouldn't be going to the dance), but she felt like she needed a special boost today. As she admired herself in the mirror, she was glad she'd made the choice. The blue made her red hair sparkle and brought out the color of her sea-foam eyes. She got out her tube of Max Factor Strawberry Meringue, a pastel pearly pink lipstick that she saved for special occasions. She wanted to wear her white kitten heels, but it was before Memorial Day and she wouldn't be caught dead in white shoes (*tell Bev that*, she thought as an image of Bev's white tennis shoes came to mind). Her little black flats would just have to do.

She even asked Nana for a ride to school; she felt like Queen Elizabeth II herself and she didn't want to arrive all sweaty and wilted after a long walk in the sun and before the day had even begun.

Mary knew that she would get some eyeballs wearing her new dress, but she hadn't expected the whispering and mocking. In between each class, she'd run to the bathroom to make sure there wasn't a stain or a sign on her back that she couldn't see. But there wasn't. It was no use; nobody noticed the glorious fabric or the perfect stitching or the detail of the rose at her waist; they just saw a passé redhead playing dress-up.

Mary was now relieved that she didn't have the same lunch period as the other girls. She knew she'd still have to see them in fifth period, but she didn't mind putting it off as long as she could, even though procrastinating was usually at the top of her list of undesirable sins. At least she was making progress; now instead of hiding in the bathroom during lunch, she'd been taking cover between the shelves of the school library.

Only today she didn't feel like she was making forward steps, even with her new beautiful frock. She felt like she was being swallowed whole. So as she sat leaning up against a stack of oversized books on the floor of the art history section, she let a quiet whimper escape. And then she couldn't stop more tears from coming. She indulged in a good cry for the second day in a row; only it didn't feel like indulging, it felt like compulsion.

That's enough, she told herself and reached for a hankie in her small handbag.

"Mary?"

She knew before looking up. It was James O'Grady. Of course is was. It was Friday the 13th; what more horrifying thing could possibly happen to her? She was sniveling on the floor and this is the moment James–not any old body, but *James O'Grady*–chose to make a jaunt to the art history section of the school library.

She quickly wiped her eyes and nose and offered a perky, "Hiya!"

"What's up? Are you OK?"

"Oh, sure. I'm swell," Mary said in her chipper-est tone. "Just a bad day. You know how it is, Friday the 13th and all." She tried to make light of it.

"Actually, I forgot it was Friday the 13th," James said, sitting down next to her, much to her chagrin. He had a thick art book in his hands, and put it on the floor on his other side. "Hey, killer dress, by the way," he said in an effort to cheer her.

"Thanks," she said taking it as a compliment. "I actually made it." She had to blow her nose again.

He ignored her runny nose and said, "You made it? That's pretty sweet. The color makes me think: *And they were canopied by the blue sky, so cloudless, clear, and purely beautiful, that God alone was to be seen in Heaven."*

Mary stared at him.

"Lord Byron," James said, suddenly self-conscious.

"That's wonderful," Mary breathed, and then she looked away, also self-conscious.

"Sorry. I'm a geek, remember? I like literature. Who else would wander in the school library at lunch? Oh . . . except for you, of course."

"No, it's worse than that. I'm not wandering, I'm in a heap on the floor bawling."

They glanced at each other and burst out laughing. Mary pushed away any thoughts of Ann. She would not apologize. James had found her. And she wanted to be found.

"So, why *are* you in a heap on the floor bawling?"

"I'm preparing for a dramatic role," she said, keeping a straight face.

James went right along with the lark. "What role?"

"Lady MacBeth."

"I played Lady MacBeth in the third grade," James said, with mock pride.

"Oh, I know. I saw you. You were marvelous. The best Lady MacBeth I've ever seen. Who do you think I'm modeling myself after?"

They burst out laughing again.

James hopped up and put out his hand to pull her up. "I gotta return this book and get going. Almost time for my next class."

Mary put her hand in his and let him ease her to her feet. She couldn't help but stare into his eyes. Without being able to stop the words from spilling out of her mouth she said, "Are you going to the dance tomorrow night?"

"I am if you are."

"OK." She smiled.

"And I think you should wear this dress."

Little did he know, she now wanted to wear the dress forever. She'd wear it to bed, to do house chores, to study in . . . "OK," she said again. And then she added, "Thank you."

"For what?"

"For cheering me up."

He winked. "My pleasure, Lady MacBeth."

Dear Ann,

I'm sorry if you felt I was keeping secrets from you. I never meant to hurt you and I never thought to take away something—someone—from you. I do like You-know-who, but I can't apologize for that. I don't think I can change it, either. I've tried to stop liking him, but I can't. I wouldn't ask you to stop liking him. But I would ask that we try to remain friends. Can we try? No more secrets, I promise.

Yours truly,

Mary

Mary was the last to walk in to fifth period and she kept her head down. She wasn't exactly confident, but she sure wasn't depressed since leaving the library. On her way to her seat, she slid the note to Ann. Ann grabbed her hand and said, "psssst . . ." and slipped a note between Mary's book and folder. She didn't make eye contact with any of the other girls.

Dear Mary,
Please forgive me for the mean things I
said to you. You have every right to like
who you like. I know better than anyone
that you can't tell your heart how to feel . . .
or not feel. I know you weren't trying to
hurt me. I only hope you will forgive me.
Your friend always,
—Ann

Mary and Ann read each other's notes at the same time. Mary tried not to well up again; her hankie was already saturated. Ann sighed a breath of relief. Finally their eyes met and they smiled and nodded. Then they looked at Judy. She questioned them silently, but their expressions showed they forgave her, too. She grinned back. Bev and Maxine even signaled each other. It felt like the thick blanket of tension in the atmosphere between them had been flung off of the whole room.

Maybe if they hadn't been so distracted, they would have noticed how despondent their teacher Mrs. Fairview was.

19

Doubleheader

It had been a roller coaster ride of a day. After an extended practice and a shower that lasted almost as long, Bev wrapped herself in her robe and headed for her room. She heard loud thumping music coming from one of the boys' rooms as usual and a TV blaring from downstairs. She'd head down to the kitchen after she was dressed and heat up some frozen-something, or make a peanut butter and jelly sandwich. But she paused in the hallway, staring at the open door at the end. Her parents' bedroom. She hadn't been in it since before.

She crept down the hall toward it, passing her room and wrapping the towel around her head. Their room was painted a tranquil bluish gray with white, brown and gray accents. It was not nearly as immaculate as in the past; their "old" room had looked like a showcase–traditional walnut furniture, gleaming from being regularly buffed and polished; a queen-sized bed quilted in a cream-colored bedspread that grazed the floor; pale green walls with a lovely landscape painting over their bed and one pastel portrait of each of their children on the walls. The curtains had matched the bedspread and a wing-back chair in the corner near the window was the same heavy cream fabric as the bedspread and curtains. Now the room seemed very modern; the bed was much bigger, and even the furniture that was meant to look traditional, like the dresser and mirror, were clearly contemporary. A desk in a corner had a lot of intimidating electronic equipment and a big flat screen and a laundry basket of clothes sat waiting for attention in the corner. On the wall, instead of pastel portraits, framed school pictures hung. Beverly went and inspected them, especially hers. But she was wearing a white oxford shirt, as were her brothers, so she couldn't get a feeling for when the picture had been taken, or bring herself to remember anything about it, just like the family portrait downstairs.

For fun, like she used to do as a kid before her mother shooed her out, she flung herself on her parents' bed. There was something so special about the adults' bedroom; maybe because she generally wasn't allowed in there. As she laid there, letting her mind wander and staring at the ceiling, she caught a whiff of her mother's perfume. She rolled over and stuffed her face into a pillow and breathed in through her nose. Chanel No. 5. It was like she was transported to another place and time; it felt like Christmas morning when she was a kid . . . full of promise, anticipation and celebration. She thought of all the days she had come home from school to be welcomed with a comforting, scented hug from her mother. She thought how every game, every school event, her parents had been there. How they managed it with five ankle-biters, she never thought to question. She longed for that time . . . not just her childhood, but that era.

Gary came out of his room and glanced down the hall. He noticed Bev with her head buried in their mom's pillow, curled up on their parents' bed. He went to join her, laying on their dad's side.

"Big game . . . or should I say games . . . tomorrow," he said.

"Um-hmmmm," Bev said from the depths of the feather pillow.

"Whatcha doin'?" He laughed.

"Smelling Mom's perfume." She rolled over. "Since I never get to see her, I thought it might be nice to at least *smell* her."

Her brother Gary was a softer version of Bob; his features weren't quite as angular and strong, but it was obvious they were brothers. All her brothers gave the appearance of being clearly related, their long-ish faces, light brown hair and hazel eyes that drooped just enough at the outer corners to make them seem sympathetic—when they weren't teasing or laughing. Gary was the only one in the family who wasn't much interested in athletics. He was a talented musician who made holidays and parties interesting with his piano playing and sparkling conversation. He was also kinder than her other brothers; even Bob, to whom she felt particularly close, had a tendency to be self-absorbed.

"Do you think she'll come to either of my games tomorrow?" Bev asked.

Gary shrugged. "They both missed my recital two weeks ago. Times are hard; she's trying to get her business off the ground and Dad's always working overtime, trying to move up in the company."

"I guess," Bev said. "I still miss them."

"I know. I'll come to all your games," he promised.

"Thanks. You're a good brother."

"Your favorite?"

"Yes, but don't tell the others." She was delighted. This was a little game they used to play, telling each other they were their favorites. "Do you think Mom's disappointed that I'm playing ball with the fellas? She always wanted me to be more . . . feminine."

Gary laughed. "You're asking me? I'm always wondering if Mom and Pops are disappointed in me for *not* playing sports."

"Maybe we should switch places," she suggested.

"OK, but I will not wear a dress," he quipped.

"I don't know if you've noticed, but neither will I! Maybe that's my problem." She thought of Conrad. It was like a timer went off in her head: *time to think of Conrad! It's been five minutes! Time to think of Conrad!*

He rolled over onto his side to face her. "Bev, promise me you won't try to change who you are . . . for anyone, not even Mom and Pops."

"What about for a boy?"

"Especially not for a boy." He wanted to ask who, but didn't. "Hey," he said, "don't tell the others, but you're my favorite sister."

She gave him a huge grin. "Heya Gary . . . I won't change if you won't."

"Deal."

On Saturday, Bev woke up refreshed and eager to play. A doubleheader! It sounded like heaven. But as she drove to the park with Bob, with her trusty ash Louisville Slugger at her side that Coach had begrudgingly agreed she could use, she realized she and the girls had never discussed the games after their little tiff with each other and she wondered wistfully if they'd show. She warmed up for an hour, and with a half hour to go before the first game, she scanned the bleachers and noted Judy, Maxine, Mary and Ann dutifully sitting in a row. They saw her looking and Judy waved frantically. Bev's eyes filled with tears as her heart filled with relief. She didn't even downplay it like she normally would; she waved right back. Then to make things even better, Gary arrived, sitting right behind Ann. But no sign of her parents yet. She had hoped to surprise them when they came for Bob's games, but they hadn't come to the first game she'd played in. Today felt different. Today it felt important that they come.

The stands began to fill with the rowdy fans and colors of the other team, the Panthers. Bev didn't mind that; it wasn't who was there that bothered her as much as who *wasn't*. Because he'd still been suspended the day before, Conrad hadn't practiced with the team. But a few minutes before the first pitch, Conrad, in uniform, emerged from the locker room and strode toward the field. Bev sucked in her breath and tried to look away. Was he walking in slow motion? She tore her gaze from him and forced herself to look into the stands. There, sitting next to Gary were Mom and Pops. Gary grinned at her. Her day had just improved a million times over.

The game was tense, a pitchers' duel with Bob on the mound facing the Panthers' League All-Star pitcher Jack Wilson. Until the sixth inning, both teams were held scoreless. Bev played shortstop and couldn't wait for the ball to come to her. She had kept her focus, but to do that, she'd had to steer clear of Conrad, even managing to keep him out of her line of sight. She caught one infield pop-up to support her brother's so-far perfect game. She was elated that her parents got to see Bob in action.

The trouble came at the top of the sixth when the Panthers were up to bat. Just before running onto the field, Conrad grabbed Bev's arm.

"Hey, good catch last inning, Jenkins. And thanks for having my back the other day. You know, talking to Coach."

"No sweat," she said. And suddenly, everything felt loosey-goosey and her joints went to liquid. *Focus, Bev,* she told herself. But now instead of the game, all her mind was filled with was *Conrad Marshall.* She tried to breathe, tried to concentrate; she prayed the ball wouldn't come to her until she got her focus back. But corralling her thoughts was like herding wild cats–not a good sign since they were playing the *Panthers.*

With a struggle, Bob managed to strike out the first two batters. The Panthers' big hitter, first baseman Vincent Schultz, was up next. The atmosphere intensified, usually a sensation that Bev fed off of. She knew she and the other fielders needed to back Bob up now more than ever. On the second pitch, Schultz hit a sharp ground ball right to Bev. Her heart racing, she snapped up the ball and hurled it toward first base, throwing it wide, and Schultz advanced to second. Bob briefly hung his head, but they tried to shake it off, knowing their weakest hitter was up next.

"It's OK, it's a'ight," Conrad encouraged the team from the outfield.

Oh, shut up, please stop talking, Bev begged silently at the sound of his sweet voice.

The next batter fouled off the first pitch and popped up the second. It sped over Bev's head and she felt a seed of panic sprout. She backed up; though she clearly heard Conrad call it, she couldn't stop herself from going after it, trying to make up for her last error. Conrad searched for the ball in the sun and felt the weight of it in his glove for the briefest moment before Bev backed right into him. The ball slid out of his glove and dribbled away from them.

"Sorry!" Bev whimpered and crouched to get it at the same time as Conrad; their heads bumped as they both leaned toward it. Nervous laughter rippled through the stands.

"Jenkins," hissed Conrad. She was still scrambling, in his way. Finally, "*Beverly!*"

She froze and he recovered the ball, heaving it to Duncan at home plate, but it was too late. Schultz had scored a run and their "weak hitter" was now standing smugly on second base. Bev could feel the exasperation radiating from Conrad as he backed away from her, shaking his head. Her face burned and she swallowed the urge to cry.

Bob struck out the next batter, stranding the Panthers' runner on second. The Rams and their fans breathed a sigh of relief at getting out of the inning and allowing only one run.

Bev wasn't able to redeem herself when she was up to bat only a few moments later at the bottom of the sixth. She swung at everything and struck out. The team wasn't mad at her; worse, they simply disregarded her. At the bottom of the seventh, the Rams second baseman hit a double and Conrad followed it with a home run. The Rams beat the Panthers 2-1, with no help from Bev.

She felt like she was trying to breathe underwater; she was slated to pitch the second game. The Panthers seemed pretty confident that they could beat the Rams since the Rams would have a girl on the mound–one that had just proved she was easily rattled–and Bev was worried that her team agreed with their opponents.

She didn't have long to warm up to pitch, but took a moment to approach Conrad.

She could barely speak. "I'm sorry, Conrad. I'm so sorry . . . ."

He looked at her hard. He didn't seem angry, but he was serious. "You know they think they can beat us with you on the mound."

"I know."

"Can they?"

"I hope not."

"You gotta do better than hoping," Conrad said. "Do you like it when people think you can't do something because you're a girl?"

"No, I hate it."

"OK, then, prove 'em wrong."

He flicked the rim of her baseball cap, then winked at her and walked away straightening his own hat.

As she watched him strut away, she felt the snap . . . that adjustment deep down where suddenly the universe felt aligned. The game was hers and she knew it.

After she warmed up, Coach put his arm around her shoulder. "You can do this, Jenkins. We all have confidence in you. Put the last game behind you; your team needs you. Remember, on that hill, you're not a boy or a girl; you're our pitcher. You got it?"

"Yeah, Coach," she said and gave him a confident smile.

"OK, let's do this," he encouraged. She headed toward the mound.

The sun was getting lower in the sky and the edges of everything shimmered in gold. *Remember this moment,* she told herself. *You traveled fifty-five years in time, somehow, to arrive at this moment.* She didn't know what it all meant, but she knew she was up to it, knew it was just for her. She tossed the ball to Marsalis. He recognized the look of determination in her eye and he smirked at her. He was looking forward to seeing her beat those cocky Panthers.

From the stands, she heard Diane Dunkelman call out, "Bring back the other Jenkins!" and her friends chuckled with her. It was just what Bev needed and she took it as a dare.

The first inning flew by; Bev pitched on adrenaline, striking out three in a row. She knew for the first inning she had the element of surprise, but for the rest of the game, she'd need more than adrenaline and a girl's name to beat these guys.

In the third inning, she allowed two runs and her team answered with two. In the fifth inning, the Rams allowed another run with two outs. Bev looked into the bleachers. The whole game, her friends' enthusiasm hadn't waned. Even Mary, the quietest of them all, was screaming encouragement, drowning out the sound of Diane Dunkelman's guffaws, snorts and derisive comments. Bev stifled a laugh when she glimpsed Judy cast a dirty eyeball at Diane.

The next batter hit a deep fly ball to Conrad, who caught it easily for the third out. They jogged to the dugout.

Bev stepped up to the plate. She drove her right foot into the dirt and slowed her breathing. After reaching for an outside pitch, she hit a ground ball down the line, over first base and past Schultz for a double. She liked how it felt to wipe the sneer off their pitcher's face. But she didn't feel arrogant, she just felt like herself, like she was playing with her brothers and Pops in the backyard. Baseball felt fun again.

Marsalis got on first and after him, Bob was up. He hit the back fence, giving Bev enough time to dig in, round third and score the tying run. The crowd went wild; all except for Diane Dunkelman, who remained noticeably quiet and even sullen, even though it was Bob who got the RBI.

In the last inning, Bev walked the first batter, struck out the next two and allowed another run. Refusing to crumble, she steeled her resolve, kept her focus and got them out of the inning and up to bat.

In the stands, Maxine was filled with pride watching her friend Bev and her cousin Conrad. Uncle TJ sat a few rows behind her and they caught each other's eye, cheering and laughing.

Judy's mood was much improved, not only because she enjoyed seeing Bev and Bob play, but because she was amused by Diane Dunkelman's visible envy of Bev's being in the spotlight.

Ann and Mary both noted James, who was sitting with a friend several rows away. He waved to both of them and they waved back. When he returned his attention to the game, Ann sighed, "He's adorable."

"Dreamy," Mary agreed. And they dissolved into giggles. Somehow it just didn't feel as devastating to like the same fellow as they had previously thought.

At the bottom of the last inning–the seventh, since it was a doubleheader–the Rams were down a run 4-3, but there was a feeling of hope sweeping through the crowd. They had the momentum: that special confidence that comes with a certain magic in the air. But even the excitement and optimism charging the atmosphere didn't mean that the Rams didn't still have to give it all they had.

With two outs, Bob was up to bat. The crowd was on its feet, and those who weren't holding their breath were using it all up screaming his name and words of encouragement. With a full count, Bob swung with all his force, grazing the ball enough for it to dribble down the third base line. He tore to first base, and was called safe by an eyelash. The Panthers' coach didn't agree and ran out to "talk" to the first base ump. The crowd booed, not willing to give up their last chance at a win. Then Coach Riggins jogged out to join in the debate. After a conversation that seemed to last hours, the Panthers' coach finally shrugged in frustration and the call stood: Bob was safe on first.

Conrad was up. The air felt electric. He knew it was all in his hands and he wouldn't have it any other way. The spectators in the stands were going hoarse barking out cheers and whistling, stomping and clapping. His fellow team members in the dugout were on their feet leaning toward him. It all hung in the balance; this play determined if they would advance to the district championship game.

First pitch: a fast ball down the middle. He swung and felt the emptiness of swinging at nothing but air. Strike one. He reminded himself he didn't have to try to hit every ball thrown in his general direction. But that *was* a good pitch. He took the next one, but unfortunately it was a good pitch, too. Strike two. A collective groan rumbled through the fans. In the briefest instant, his concentration broke and he thought of pulling the fire alarm the other day before fifth period. He'd done it to be funny; he knew he'd be caught and he'd wanted the attention. He got some alright, and the most unexpected attention he'd gotten was Maxine's rant and Beverly Jenkins's plea to the coach behind his back to let him play. He adjusted his batting glove, touched the rim of his batting helmet. This was the attention he really wanted and this was the way to thank Maxine, his dad, and his team, including Bev.

He felt the world slow to half time, then quarter time. He watched the ball leave the pitcher's fingers, watched it float right toward him. He swore he saw his name printed on it. Without thinking–just knowing, just feeling–he felt the bat pull away from his shoulder and plunge toward the ball, his shoulders and arms jolt satisfyingly with the impact of bat meeting ball . . . .

Conrad didn't remember running the bases, but he must have, and he must have tagged them all because the team leaped joyfully on him, smothering him, while the crowd screamed with new energy.

Bev was among them; jumping, yelling, hugging her teammates. Soon the spectators had joined them all on the field to celebrate. She didn't even care when Diane Dunkelman came to congratulate her brother. Of course maybe she didn't mind because Diane got to hear Coach say to Bob, "You got another sister? I'd like to have one more Jenkins to take to State." And then Coach grabbed Bev by the shoulders and told her how proud he was.

As Bev made her way to Conrad, her parents and Gary intercepted her. They hugged her and bubbled over with compliments. Gary insisted she got all her athletic ability from him. She gave him a hug and whispered, "You stink at baseball, but you're still my favorite brother. Don't tell the others."

By the time the hype had died down, she saw Conrad talking to his dad and Maxine and didn't want to interrupt a family conversation. Maybe she'd see him at the dance tonight and she could congratulate him then.

20

Rock Around the Clock

Mary straightened her dress and looked at herself in the mirror. Behind her, the Singer reflected one gleam of bright light that made it look like it was sitting in a showcase display. She smiled at herself, and even though it felt silly, she silently thanked her sewing machine for helping her find a few moments of peace . . . and for helping her make this beautiful dress that James said reminded him of the sky.

This predicament they were in, this parallel universe . . . she was beginning to think it wasn't so terrible. And maybe tonight, just for once, she would stop being such a wet blanket worrying about Nancy-Drew-clues and meaning and lessons. Maybe tonight she'd just enjoy herself.

Judy had only a few minutes before her mom was going to drop her off at the school dance. Bitsy was on her way to yet another date with her boss, Roger Streeter, and for once, Judy couldn't have cared less. She flipped through her autograph book and thought how she should have Bev sign it now that she was practically famous for being a girl baseball player. Of course, Bob would have to sign it, too. Her heart sank a little as she thought of that wretched Diane Dunkelman.

She realized with a start that she hadn't thought of her friend Susan in days. She hadn't meant to be disloyal, but she was finally feeling like she wasn't alone after all. She had friends right here and right . . . *now.*

Judy turned to the first page in her book and gazed at her daddy's signature and message. He had signed it, "Love Always." And in that moment, sitting on her bed in her poodle skirt, she felt his love. Even above the disappointment surrounding Diane and Bob. It occurred to her how fun it would be to have all the girls, the Fifties Chix, sign her book. It would remind her of their adventures in this strange dimension, even if they were to go back to 1955, which she was starting to not want at all.

"Love always," she said quietly to herself.

Maxine knew that the dance would probably be a lot more appealing if she were interested in a boy. As she smoothed her skirt, which she rarely wore except to church, she reminded herself that she *was* interested in a boy. Kind of, but not in *that* way. She was interested to know if James had read her essay. She was interested to know if it would be published in the next *Invisible Truth*. She still had the ink stains on her hands, and even the little dent where the quill had cut into her middle finger. She had been tempted to feel guilty about not doing enough to figure out when, where and why she and the girls had woken up this way; but Maxine's exhilaration at pouring her heart out in words, using her great-grandmother's quill no less, far outshone any guilt. Plus she wasn't entirely sure she was ready to solve this mystery after all. At least not before her essay was published.

Ann could not believe her ears.

"Darling, if you had told us you already had plans, we would have arranged it for a different time." Mrs. Branislav tried to soothe her daughter.

"But tonight of all nights? It could be any other time, but not tonight." She knew her voice was shrill, but she couldn't help it. She'd come home after the doubleheader to change for the dance and meet the girls, and her mother had announced that they had dinner plans to celebrate her mother's new business deal. All week she had craved some semblance of family time, and now when she just wanted to be with her friends, out of nowhere, her mother was demanding it. Would Ann ever experience any justice? She told herself to not have a cow, tried to calm herself, but it wasn't working.

Now her mother spoke to her sharply. "Anna, you can go to the dance after dinner. It's not going to kill you to spend time with your family. Besides, we're meeting the Jenkins. I'm sure Beverly will be there. Maybe you two can escape early to go to the dance."

It was about the only thing that could possibly placate Ann. Finally consenting, she went to her room to dress, slipping on a gray pencil skirt that went below her knees and a dark pink and white striped blouse with a large white collar. She put her fake pearl necklace on and donned a straw and pink-ribboned hat. She took a moment to gaze at her painting, which was coming along bit by bit every day. She stroked the barrel of her favorite paintbrush before closing her bedroom door behind her.

When they arrived at the restaurant, the first time Ann had ever gone to a restaurant with her parents (since they had always only gone to Klein's Kosher Café), Mr. and Mrs. Jenkins sat at a table with Bev and one of their sons, Gary. Bev looked about as happy to be there as Ann, but their eyes lit up when they saw each other. As the families greeted one another, Mrs. Jenkins apologized that her other sons could not have come; she explained they all had plans she didn't know about, including Bob who had a date. Ann and Bev rolled their eyes at each other at this and Gary caught sight of them and smirked.

The first few moments of the gathering, Mr. Jenkins bragged about his daughter's baseball game, while his wife smiled next to him. He said, "We haven't been to all of her games, but we're sure glad we made this one."

He smiled proudly and reached across the table to playfully tug on Bev's earlobe. She grinned back, though she looked uncomfortable. Ann couldn't believe it, but Bev was in a dress. It was an aqua, green and white plaid cotton frock with a full skirt. If Bev hadn't been so fidgety and seemed so awkward about it, she might have looked beautiful. Her hair was even down; Ann hadn't thought Bev's hair knew any other way to be than in a pony tail.

The conversation very quickly turned to business and the girls grew bored; even Ann's initial awe of being out at a "regular" restaurant with such expensive prices wore off as she thought of being at the dance instead. Ann and Bev whispered and chatted, biding their time until they could escape to meet the other girls. They kept asking Gary what time it was and they knew the other girls would be at the dance by now. Finally, Gary interrupted the adults to ask if it would be alright if he and the girls excused themselves.

When Ivan and Katrina saw their daughter's quiet pleading expression, they laughed and agreed. The three teens hurriedly darted for the car.

On the way to the school, Gary peppered Ann with questions, but she was distracted thinking about the other girls and wondering if she would see James tonight. She answered half-heartedly and absent-mindedly.

When they pulled up at the school, Bev said, "You can just drop us at the gym."

Gary laughed. "I know I'm just a chauffeur to you, but I go to this school, too. Mind if I come to the dance?"

"Oh, of course not," Bev tittered. In the faint evening light, she noticed some kids going inside. She touched her hair, self-conscious. *Was that Conrad? No. Shoot.*

Gary chuckled. "Dang, you two need to chill. You're nervous wrecks." He was seeing a new side of his little sister.

"Let's just park and go in," implored Bev.

The girls managed to walk with Gary and not scramble ahead of him. The gym doors opened and out poured dizzying lights and blaring music. In fact, the music was so loud, they could even feel and taste it.

"Thanks for the ride," Bev hollered at Gary.

"Welcome," he yelled back, over the music. But as the girls made their way through the crowd to find the others, Gary went with them. Bev didn't mind, but Ann hoped James wouldn't see her with another boy and get the wrong idea.

"There they are!" Ann shrieked, pointing.

In the far corner of the gym, pressed together like frightened kittens, Maxine, Judy and Mary huddled. They had all dressed up: Judy wore her favorite poodle skirt, Mary had again donned her pretty new blue dress, and Maxine's dark navy skirt was a rare site. They spotted Bev and Ann and brightened, waving madly so the two wouldn't miss them, even though they were already on their way over.

They hugged and squealed, not sure why they were so excited. This wasn't exactly their scene and it was nothing like they'd expected. There was no attempt to disguise the gym with signs or decorations; the Christmas dance had been well-lit and festive with greenery, banners and lots of student committee-made decorations. There was dancing, but there was also plenty of room to enjoy a cup of punch and have a pleasant conversation. Tonight, the music was too loud for conversation, the flashing colored lights were disorienting, and the air felt hot and humid with so many bodies crammed into one place.

"This is my brother, Gary." Bev introduced her brother at the top of her lungs.

"Hi, I'm her *favorite* brother," Gary joked.

"What?" a couple of the girls hollered.

Ann heard him, though, and giggled.

Seeing Gary reminded Judy of Bob. "Has anyone seen him?" She searched the crowd. Which got Ann, Mary and Bev also searching the crowd, but not for Bob.

"Wooohoooo!" They heard a celebratory whoop and saw the catcher, Duncan Marsalis, run toward Bev.

"Jenkins! Good game!" He lifted her up and spun her around.

"Good game, yourself, Dunc," Bev said, again touching her hair nervously as he set her down. Duncan's accolades drew some attention to Bev and soon there was a small crowd circling her offering praise and congratulations. She looked like she would rather be anywhere other than the center of attention while wearing a dress.

The music continued to pound on and the astonished girls watched the other kids dance. There were no couples, really, just globs of folks dancing individually, occasionally bumping into each other. The girls looked at each other and shook their heads, stunned.

"There's my cousin!" Maxine said, spotting Conrad coming in the gym doors. "I'm going to go say hi."

"Can I come?" Bev asked.

Then right behind Conrad and two of his friends, Bob and Diane Dunkelman entered.

"Oh, can I come, too?" Judy asked.

"Let's all go," Maxine said.

"No, I can wait . . . ." Bev vacillated.

But like a single unit, the five girls started moving toward the opposite corner of the gym. Kids noticed as they made their way through the crowd not only because of how they were dressed, but because they appeared to be comically tethered together by some invisible force.

Maxine threw her arms around her cousin, making up for having hidden from him in the bathroom the previous week. "I'm so proud of you," she gushed for the twelfth time since the end of the game. The girls all looked at him and smiled in agreement, except for Judy, who appeared to be gazing *through* him to Bob and Diane, who had been stopped by one of Bob's teammates. And Bev, who was staring at the floor.

"You," Conrad said, getting Bev's attention.

"Oh, hiya," she said, as if noticing him for the first time.

"Good game." He chucked her gently on the shoulder.

The girls all peered at Bev . . . was she *blushing*? She played with her hair, tucked it behind her ear, untucked it and put it back again. "It was all you," Bev insisted.

"Oh, no, it wasn't. *I* can't pitch like that."

"It was far from a perfect game," she argued.

"You'll get your shot," he came back. Suddenly they were bantering like there wasn't anyone else in the room.

"Thanks for your help," Bev said, letting herself look into his eyes. A luxury she would allow herself as a reward for winning the game.

"Thanks for yours," Conrad said. To this she looked down, shyly.

"Hey," he added. "You clean up good, Jenkins." He grinned a sincere smile, bearing his gorgeous white teeth and showcasing his dimples. Bev was saved by the kids who came up to clap Conrad on the back. Her knees were on the verge of buckling and she could feel her heart beating all the way up in her eyeballs.

"There she is!" Bob reached through the crowd to Bev. "The best pitcher in the family!" The crowd shifted and he gave her a half hug. His other half hug was bestowed on Diane Dunkelman, who seemed to be glued to his hip. On Bev's other side, Judy materialized out of thin air.

"Great games, Bob!" she enthused, trying to ignore the other blonde in his life.

"Thanks, Judy. Thanks for coming." He glanced at her clothes, and it made him look at what the other girls were wearing, too.

Diane Dunkelman sneered. "OMG. I *told you. The Fifties Chix.*" She attempted a whisper in his ear, but of course, no one could whisper in this place, so she was actually bellowing for all to hear.

He laughed. "Yeah, I know. Cool, isn't it?" He winked at his sister and Diane Dunkelman looked like she had eaten a bug.

"Let's go dance," Diane sniffed.

"Bye, Bob!" Judy called and when he had passed them, her face fell.

"Don't worry," Maxine soothed. "*That's* temporary." She jerked her thumb in Diane Dunkelman's direction.

"Oh, do you really think so?" Judy said eagerly.

The girls all nodded in agreement. Judy perked up slightly.

Suddenly, Ann grabbed Mary's hand. Mary followed her gaze and saw James heading right for them. The two of them froze. What would they do? Who would he talk to? With smiles plastered on their faces, they prepared to greet him, but he almost seemed to not notice.

"Beverly!" he said, putting his fist up. Bev had seen her teammates do this and had learned the hard way: she put her fist up and he bumped it with his. "Sweet game! You rocked! I'd love to talk to you about Title Nine and what it's like to be a woman on the guys' team sometime."

Slightly unnerved, and overly conscious of her two besotted friends ogling him, she agreed noncommittally. Then he did something very curious and looked at Maxine. He gave her a thumbs up and a nod. From that point on, Maxine couldn't stop beaming.

Just when Ann and Mary were going to ask Maxine what was going on after James had turned away, he spun back around. "Oh, hi, Ann. And nice dress, Mary."

Before they could melt into the floor, a familiar sound blasted through the speakers: *One, two, three o'clock, four o'clock–rock!*

Involuntarily, the girls screamed and grabbed each other. Without thinking, they ran, clustered, to the dance floor and flung their shoes off. The dance floor cleared and the five of them danced as if they were at a slumber party at Judy's house. Bob and Gary stood laughing on the sidelines, while other kids stared at them, astounded, some of them jeering. Bev grabbed her brothers and they joined the sock hop, trying to mimic the girls' steps.

"Conrad!" Maxine called to her cousin and many eyes turned to him to see what he would do. He shook his head "no," but then a contingent of the students started chanting his name "Mar-*shall*, Mar-*shall*," and then he, too, tossed his shoes off and joined the dancers. James and his friend jumped in and suddenly, there was no room on the dance floor and everyone in the gym had dissolved into dancing and laughter.

The Fifties Chix were having their own sock hop right there in the gym.

This is the best night of my life, Bev thought, still high from the game.

This is the best night of my life, even though he's with her, thought Judy.

This is the best night of my life, Ann thought, glancing at James.

Seeing the joy in their friends' faces, Mary and Maxine thought the same thing.

When the music ended, no one wanted to stop dancing. The DJ spoke into the mic: "That one went out to Mrs. Fairview, who announced she is retiring after fifty-eight years of teaching here!" Everyone applauded. "To the former Miss Boggs, we love you!" Cheers rose again and the DJ proceeded to put more music on to keep the party going.

The room shifted. The girls froze. They stared at each other in a daze.

How had they missed the fact that all along, Miss Boggs was with them as her older self named Mrs. Fairview?

This changed everything.

21

Once in a Lifetime

May Boggs rubbed her temples. She never should have told Reggie she wouldn't go to dinner with him. She had the weekend to grade papers. Her mother had warned her about becoming a career girl; she had told her to always put a man first. May turned the TV off. She couldn't concentrate with I Love Lucy on. If she had declined Reggie's invitation to work then, by golly, she needed to honestly work.

But even with the television off, it was hard to concentrate on the stack of Travel to Tomorrow reports in front of her. Not only were the students' efforts dismal, she couldn't keep her mind off of charming Reginald Fairview. Besides the fact that he was everything her mother wanted for her–handsome, educated and from a good wealthy family–he was everything May herself dared not ask for. He was kind, thoughtful and supportive of her teaching career. He had already told her that if they ever were to marry, he'd never ask her to stop teaching if that's what she wanted to do.

May gazed dreamily out into the evening, through the lacy curtains she'd put up in her apartment a few months ago. Maybe this weekend he would ask her. She would say yes, of course. Mrs. Marion Gertrude Fairview. She mentally savored what her new name would be. She mused about dropping the Gertrude . . . How about Mrs. Marion B. Fairview? She loved it. Her heart leapt.

But with her line of work she needed to be careful. No personal attachments. That's why her apartment was so empty of treasures, knickknacks, or anything sentimental. She walked a fine line with Reggie. The fact that he didn't mind her teaching career, well, maybe it meant he could deal with her other calling. . . .

With a sigh, and a great deal of resolve, she adjusted her cat-eye glasses and turned her attention to her students' projects. She had high hopes for Mary Donovan, Judy White, Maxine Marshall, Beverly Jenkins and Anna Branislav. They each had such interesting backgrounds and unique perspectives; in fact, they actually inspired her idea for the Travel to Tomorrow project. She hoped their reports were better than their presentations earlier today. When they were in front of the class, May had wondered if they had understood at all the point of the project. But seeing them after school at the five-and-dime had warmed her heart. She had made them promise to be friends in another half a century. Marion knew how fleeting youth and idealism could be; if she could do anything as an educator, she wanted to give her students hope for the future, as she and her two best friends had been given once upon a time.

Well, she was about to find out if she had given hope to those five girls . . .

After reading and re-reading the girls' papers, May carefully removed her cat-eye glasses which had gotten a little steamy. She rubbed her temples. She surmised she would have to meet them tomorrow after class, but she knew deep down this wouldn't be enough. She reminded herself of why she had become a teacher in the first place.

No, a little teacher speech wouldn't be enough for these five girls. She would have to take more extreme measures. She had mixed feelings about it . . . but she knew, in the end, their own personal "travels to tomorrow" would be for the best. It might be tough going at first, but wasn't that why she had made them promise to be friends at the soda shop earlier? It would all work in the end.

She would just keep reminding herself of this fact, no matter what happened.

She looked down at the ornate gold watch around her wrist, which she had been given for this very purpose, not that that fact made what she had to do any easier.

It was time.

Miss Boggs wound her watch and braced herself.

22

Glossary

Glossary of 1950s Terms and Fun Historical Tid-bits!

Actor: show-off, someone who makes a big display of their abilities

Ankle-biters: kids

Backseat bingo: kissing *a lot*; "making out;" see also "necking"

Beatnik/Beat: Webster's has "a young person in the 1950s and early 1960s belonging to a subculture associated with the 'beat' generation," a concept introduced by writer Jack Kerouac. The slang terms "beat" and "beatnik" referred to a "beaten down" or "lost" generation–we're still labeling generations like that today! Generation X, for example. But Jack Kerouac also intended a more positive meaning to the term "beat" which was often lost or overlooked–it referred to the Beatitudes and he had this to say in clarification: "It is because I am Beat, that is, I believe in beatitude and that God so loved the world that He gave His only begotten son to it . . . Who knows, but that the universe is not one vast sea of compassion actually, the veritable holy honey, beneath all this show of personality and cruelty?" Even with Jack Kerouac himself clarifying his own concept, there was still widespread stereotyping that a beatnik was a dark and dangerous rebel type; Author Joyce Johnson describes beats this way "[The] 'Beat Generation' sold books, sold black turtleneck sweaters and bongos, berets and dark glasses, sold a way of life that seemed like dangerous fun—thus to be either condemned or imitated."

Big tickle: so funny!

Black listing: denying someone privileges or access to a group. In 1947 the House Un-American Activities Committee (HUAC) launched an investigation into Communist influence on the motion picture industry and held hearings. Communism was and is still seen by many as unpatriotic in the US because it doesn't allow for individual freedom as the US Constitution guarantees its citizens; it prohibits a free market economy, and it gives total control to the state. Ideally, it is supposed to be about common (or communal) ownership of property, but this hasn't been achieved and instead the government ends up with more power than the individual; a frightening and disastrous state of affairs as we can see when we look at world history through the centuries. Because of the fear of the effects of Communism, the hearings and accusations of the McCarthy era (see "Communist") were reminiscent of the Salem witch trials of 1692. See more under "Soviet Union."

Bobbie Socks: white socks that girls wore folded just above their ankles. Great for sock hops, by the way.

Boss: as an adjective—good, cool, great (this word made a comeback in the 1980s.

Broken record: Instead of CDs or iTunes files, and even before cassettes, music was recorded onto vinyl disks called records. There were three different speeds on which the records played, depending on the size of the record; a whole (double-sided) record, or LP (for Long Play) played at 33, a single song (which had a flip side with one song) played at 45 (so the singles were referred to as 45s) and the even older records played at 78. Because the vinyl could be easily scratched, the records would often "skip" or get stuck in the same groove repeating the same part over and over again. So "broken record" refers to hearing or saying the same thing over and over again.

Cary Grant: a charming leading man in the movies, Cary Grant was born in England, and so has a faint British accent. He usually played in romantic comedies, and usually played a bachelor. He was handsome, smooth and dashing, witty and charming; and this says it all: Ian Fleming partially based the character of James Bond on Cary Grant! In 1955, he had appeared in Hitchcock's *To Catch a Thief* with the lovely Grace Kelly (who later became the Princess of Monaco).

Cast an eyeball: watch, look at

Cat-eye glasses: glasses that are shaped like cats' eyes, with pointed frames

Cloud nine: the best, your happy place

Clutched: DE-nied! Turned down, rejected

Color TV: TVs didn't used to be flat OR in color! Oh the horror! They originally came in what as known as a console, which was a big wooden piece of furniture to hide all the TV stuff (that's my amateur definition). In the 1950s if a family had a television set at all, it was a pretty big deal, but having one in color or having more than one in 1955 was some sort of status symbol. Needless to say, kids did NOT have TVs in their rooms!

Colored: a term used in reference to African Americans in the 1950s to reference skin tone, but also sometimes in a derogatory and disparaging way. In present day, the term is certainly not appropriate because of the way many African Americans were derided and mistreated in association with the word.

Cold War: a conflict where no bombs were dropped between the USSR/Soviet Union and the Western World/US that started after World War II and continued until the fall of the Soviet Union in 1991. The threat to both sides of nuclear annihilation, ideological tensions, propaganda, espionage and technological competition like the Space Race fueled the Cold War.

Communist: a person who advocates communism, a stateless, classless society where all the wealth is shared equally (with the assumption that all the work is also shared equally) and all decisions are made to benefit everyone equally. Instead of private ownership of goods, which is capitalistic (and a founding principle of the United States of America), goods are collectively owned. In 1950, a United States Senator from Wisconsin, Joseph McCarthy, had started a movement of paranoia, accusing Americans of being unpatriotic traitors by calling them communists. The movement was named for him, McCarthyism. For a while, he seemed to have caused the whole country to be in a state of upheaval, almost panic, as people wondered who to trust. All anyone had to do was call someone the "C" word and it was nearly as good as convicting them of a crime. Many people were "blacklisted," kept from doing their jobs or defamed simply by the unfounded accusation of another. Even though five years later, Mr. McCarthy had been formally reprimanded by the U.S. government, it would be a long time, if ever, that the country could get over sensitivity to the "C" word.

Cooties: imaginary cause of someone being totally uncool

Cubism: an innovative art movement started by Pablo Picasso in the first quarter of the 20th century where objects are depicted in paintings or sculpture from many different angles at once creating ambiguous spaces and planes (for example, a profile that shows both sides of the face)

Desi: Desi Arnaz and Lucille Ball starred in the black and white TV sitcom, *I Love Lucy* which aired October 15, 1951 to April 1,

1960 on CBS. Lucy and Desi were a married couple in real life and played married couple Lucy and "Ricky," a Cuban American singer and bandleader. The premise of the show, as IMDB puts it, is "a daffy woman constantly strives to become a star along with her bandleader husband and gets herself in the strangest situations." The show was the first to use a three-camera setup before a live studio audience, which is now the standard. It has been on the air ever since 1951; that's 58 consecutive years!! One of the best comedians of all time, Lucy inspired generations of women, including yours truly.

Dig: to "get it" or to agree

Doris Day: Famous actress who was an adorable blond, thoroughly charming, had a squeaky-clean image; got her start singing on the radio and dancing (although an injury forced her to give up dancing for a living). She was in 39 films and lives today in Carmel CA, where she runs an inn and is an animal advocate. Fun facts: She reportedly did not like "swear words." As a recording artist, she would require anyone who said a swear word to put a quarter in a "swear jar." In addition, she does not allow her songs to be used in movies that contain swear words. She has often cited *Calamity Jane* (1953) as her personal favorite of the 39 films she appeared in.

Drag: a bummer

Dragnet: Judy's cat, Dragnet, is named for the TV show of the same title which aired on NBC on Thursday nights starting in 1952. Lead character Sgt. Joe Friday was played by creator Jack

Webb; he created the police drama to be a realistic look at police work and is known for his business-like phrase, "just the facts, Ma'am." There was a Dragnet movie in 1954 and remakes and revivals all the way into the 1980s.

Drop Dead Twice (or DDT): even worse than "drop dead;" get out of one's life, already!

Earthbound: reliable, dependable, predictable

Eisenhower; President Eisenhower: Dwight David "Ike" Eisenhower was elected President in 1953 as the 34th US President, and served 2 terms (until 1961). He was very well-known because he was Supreme Commander of the Allied forces in Europe during World War II and led the successful invasion of France and Germany in 1944-45. As President-elect, he went to Korea to find out how a conflict there could be ended; and a cease-fire was established on July 27, 1953, and so a demilitarized zone (DMZ) was established which is to this day still defended by North Korean troops on one side and South Korean and American troops on the other. President Eisenhower also kept up the pressure on the Soviet Union during the Cold War, made nuclear weapons a higher defense priority, launched the Space Race, enlarged the Social Security program started by President Roosevelt, and began the Interstate Highway System. Ike & his wife Mamie in many ways epitomized the 1950s with their clean cut image and all-American lifestyle.

Fat city: so very cool

Five-and-dime: the original "department" store sold everything from hardware to clothes to souvenirs and knickknacks and had ice cream counters where you could buy a shake, a soda or even a burger. In 1998, the last most famous five-and-dime, Woolworths, closed their doors for good. Almost every town had one at the heart of downtown. Target, KMart and Walmart stores are all modeled after the original five-and-dime–called that for the discount–and arguably led to Woolworth's closing their doors.

Fracture: to amuse no end

Fream: a freak or misfit

Frosted: angry

Georgia O'Keefe: an American woman painter who got her training in the School of Art Institute in Chicago and then the Art Students League in New York in 1905 and 1907. By the 1920s, she was making a name for herself and by the 1950s, she was living and painting in New Mexico. She painted flowers, landscapes and natural objects with a beautiful fluid style; her paintings are abstract and representational at the same time. At a time when Europe was producing great artists, Georgia O'Keefe appeared on the scene as not only a great woman artist, but an American master.

Go Ape: to freak out (go bananas!)

Goof: a clown or a fool; someone who messes up a lot

Goner: someone who is real gone= totally in love or crazy (or both)

Greaser: a guy who wore a lot of product in his hair (that looked like grease, but it was usually VO5 brand hairdressing); it came to be a term used for the bad boys.

Grody: this word was popular in the 80s, but it's actually from the 50s; it means "gross, like really gross, man."

Hat: when ladies went out, especially to church, they wore white gloves and a nice hat. Men always wore hats—called Fedoras. But men take their hats off indoors while ladies are allowed to keep them on

Hang: to chill, hang out

Have a Cow: to freak out

Hep: get it ("hep to it") or someone who gets it ("she's hep to it" or "he's hep")

Hip: hip, cool

Horn: phone ("get on the horn" = "make a phone call")

Hoover: name brand of a vacuum often used as a verb (to Hoover means to vacuum); or as a noun referring to a vacuum cleaner in general

Hullywo d: The Hollywood sign has undergone various stages of disrepair; when erected in 1923 it read "Hollywoodland." The letters spelling "land" were removed and in 1955, the top of the first "o" was missing as well as the last entire "o." For an interesting history and perspective on this iconic sign, visit http://www.hollywoodsign.org

Humphrey Bogart: a dreamy actor who was the star of the classic 1942 movie *Casablanca*

Illuminations: bright ideas

In orbit: in the know

Jack Kerouac: see "Beatnik"

James Dean: a young actor in the 1950s, who even today has a huge fan base. According to the James Dean website, he "had one of the most spectacularly brief careers of any screen star." In just more than a year, and in only three films, Dean became a widely admired screen personality, a personification of the restless American youth of the mid-50's, and an embodiment of the title of one of his film *Rebel Without A Cause*. En route to compete in a race in Salinas, California, James Dean was killed in a highway accident on September 30, 1955. He was nominated for two Academy Awards, for his performances in *East of Eden* and *Giant*. Although he only made three films, they were made in just over one year's time. Joe Hyams, in the James Dean biography *Little Boy Lost*, sums up his career: ". . . There is no simple explanation for why he has come to mean so much to so many people today. Perhaps it is because, in his acting, he had the intuitive talent for expressing the hopes and fears that are a part of all young people . . . In some movie magic way, he managed to dramatize brilliantly the questions every young person in every generation must resolve."

Jets: brains or smarts

John Wayne: John Wayne was one of the biggest movie stars of all time, and really hit his stride in the 1950s and didn't slow down from there. Ronald Reagan (in 1979, two years before he was President of the United States), had this to say about John Wayne, who was known as Duke: "For an incredible 25 years he was rated at or around the top in box-office appeal. His films grossed $700 million-a record no performer in Hollywood has come close to matching. Yet John Wayne was more than an actor; he was a force around which films were made....During the Depression he played in grade-B westerns until [director] John Ford finally convinced United Artists to give him the role of the Ringo Kid in his classic film Stagecoach. John Wayne was on the road to stardom. He quickly established his versatility in a variety of major roles..." Reagan went on to say that when [World War II] broke out, Duke wanted to enlist, but due to his age (34), an football old injury, and the fact that he was a father of four, he was rejected by the Navy. He ended up making movies and going on tours to see the troops; his activities inspired Americans everywhere. He did not get critically recognized for his acting until 1969, when he won a Best Actor Academy Award for his role in the classic Western film "True Grit." Many think that Oscar was a nod to all his films. He became the icon of the Western. When John Wayne died on June 11, 1979, a Tokyo newspaper ran the headline, "Mr. America passes on."

Kill: to impress supremely

Kookie or Kooky: crazy, nuts

Korea: Korean War, or "Conflict": In the summer of 1950, communist North Korea invaded South Korea and brought about a United Nations "police action" which meant heavy involvement for the United States. Since World War II had only ended five years before, the US still had trained military and ample supplies, but did not expect that the Korean conflict would last as long as three years. China & the USSR got involved supporting their Communist ally, North Korea. As noted in the section on President Eisenhower, a cease-fire was established on July 27, 1953 and a demilitarized zone was established which is to this day still defended by North Korean troops on one side and South Korean and American troops on the other. However, a little known fact is that a peace treaty was never actually signed and so officially speaking, the Korean war is still not ended to this day!

Make the scene: show up or attend

Mamie's Million Dollar Fudge (recipe): Mamie Eisenhower was born Mamie Doud to a wealthy family; she and her three sisters grew up in a large house with several servants. She made a very popular First Lady because of her charm, femininity, style, and her obvious pride in her husband and her home. She was known as a "penny pincher" who clipped coupons for the White House staff. Her recipe for "Mamie's million dollar fudge" was reproduced by housewives all over the country after it was printed in many publications. Mamie was not known for her culinary prowess, however, she did earn fame for her fudge, which Ike named and often enjoyed. This became a staple at the conclusion of formal White House meals and was an inexpensive treat. Here's the recipe:

Mamie's Million Dollar Fudge *Ingredients*

* *4-1/2 cups sugar*
* *2 tablespoons butter*
* *1 pinch of salt*
* *1 tall can evaporated milk*
* *12 ounces semisweet chocolate bits*
* *12 ounces German sweet chocolate*
* *1 pint marshmallow cream*
* *2 cups chopped nutmeats*

Heat the sugar, butter, salt, and evaporated milk over low heat, stirring until the sugar dissolves. Bring to a boil and boil for 6 minutes. Put chocolate bits, German chocolate, marshmallow cream, and nutmeats in a bowl. Pour the boiling syrup over the ingredients. Beat until the chocolate is all melted, then pour in a pan.

Let stand for a few hours before cutting. Remember it is better the second day. Store in a tin box.

Marilyn Monroe: when I was a teenager, I was slightly obsessed with Marilyn Monroe–whose real name was Norma Jeane Baker. She was and still is a controversial and mesmerizing woman. She had a troubled youth and soap opera kind of adulthood. Her beauty and innocence, coupled with a racy reputation made her the epitome of "blond bombshell;" she set the standard for "movie star" for all time to come. She was married for nine months to Joe DiMaggio, one of best baseball players of all time and a New York Yankee. After Joe (who it is said never stopped loving her and had white roses delivered to her grave twice a week for twenty years), Marilyn was married to Arthur Miller, one of the best playwrights of all time. She became involved with President John F. Kennedy and his brother, Attorney General Robert Kennedy. When she died of an apparent drug overdose in 1962, there were many, including Joe DiMaggio, who were convinced the Kennedys had her killed or were somehow involved with her death. So even her death is controversial and has kept interest in Marilyn Monroe alive decades after she left us. In fact, even in 1999, People magazine dubbed her "The Sexiest Woman of the Century"

Mod: short for modern, but also implies stylish

Natalie Wood: in 1955, Natalie (born Natalia to Russian immigrant parents) was 16 years old and making the transition from child start to actress. As a child, she starred in 20 movies, but 1955 saw her star with James Dean in the movie *Rebel without a*

Cause, where she earned herself a nomination for the Academy Award for Best Supporting Actress and a Golden Globe Award for Most Promising New Star

Necking: making out, kissing

Pad: house, home

Party Pooper: someone who ruins a party, a "wet blanket"

Parve: a Hebrew term that refers to a food item considered to be "neutral" by Jewish dietary law, meaning the food contains neither dairy nor meat

Pancake makeup: a very thick, usually flesh-colored cream used as a foundation; because it is thick, it covers all manner of blemishes, but it also looks like what it is: thick makeup

Peepers: eye glasses

Radioactive: popular, hot, desirable

Rattle one's cage: to get all out of sorts, disturbed or upset

Razzes your berries: have a crush on, like a lot

Real gone: Totally in love (crazy); see "Goner"

Record player: a device, before stereo systems, that played vinyl records and projected the sound into the room.

Red: a Communist, a big insult in the 1950s; used ignorantly, it could refer to any foreigner, but especially someone from Eastern Europe, like Ann.

Rollers: many girls and women put their hair in curlers or rollers every night and put a sleeping cap on over them and slept that way. Flat irons, curling irons and hand-held hair dryers weren't an option yet

Roosevelt: There were two President Roosevelts who both served long before the 1950s, but their terms of office directly influenced how Americans lived their lives in the 1950s and beyond. Theodore Roosevelt (for whom the Teddy Bear is named) served as the 26th US President from 1901, when as Vice President, the 42-year-old Roosevelt succeeded President William McKinley after McKinley's assassination. He was President until 1909. TR's niece Eleanor Roosevelt married her cousin from another side, and Theodore Roosevelt's fifth cousin, Franklin Delano Roosevelt. FDR, as he is often known, was 32nd President and the only President ever to be elected to four terms. FDR only served a few months of his fourth term before passing away unexpectedly, serving as President from 1933 until 1945. Not long after his death, the Twenty-Second Amendment was ratified in 1951, stating that "no person shall be elected to the office of President more than twice…" Both President Roosevelts were popular. FDR led the US out of the Great Depression and through World War II. There were a lot of high schools named after one of the two Roosevelts in the 1950s because there was a lot of expansion and development of new neighborhoods; a lot of growth in general can be attributed to the industrious progress achieved after World War II, in thanks to many of Franklin Roosevelt's programs and policies

Saddle shoes: classic Oxford two-color shoes with laces; usually white and black or white and dark red

Sock hop: a dance; because school dances were held in the cafeteria or the gym, attendants usually had to take off their shoes to protect the varnished floor and end up dancing in their socks

Sounds: slang for music

Soviet Union, USSR: Wikipedia has this helpful overview of what is now Russia: "the Soviet Union was founded (1922) under Joseph Stalin, who ... established the character of communism as the totalitarian ideology it is known as today [and] the Soviet Union emerged as a new global superpower on the victorious side of World War II. In the five years after the World War, communist regimes were established in many states of Central and Eastern Europe (see Yugoslavia, below) and in China. Communism began to spread its influence in the Third World while continuing to be a significant political force in many Western countries. International relations between Soviets and the West, led by USA, quickly worsened after the end of the war and the Cold war began, a continuing state of conflict, tension and competition between the United States and the Soviet Union and those countries' respective allies. The "Iron curtain" between West and East then divided Europe and world from the mid-1940s to the early 1990s. Despite many communist successes like the victorious Vietnam War (1959-1975) or the first human spaceflight (1961), the communist regimes were ultimately unable to keep up with the West....After 1985, the last Soviet leader Mikhail Gorbachev tried to implement market and democratic reforms under devices like perestroika ("restructuring") and glasnost ("transparency"). His reforms sharpened internal conflicts in the communist regimes and quickly led to the Revolutions of 1989 and a total collapse of European communist regimes outside of the Soviet Union, which dissolved itself two years later (1991)

Tatty: Yiddish term for "Daddy"

The most: the coolest thing ever

Thurgood: Thurgood Marshall was the first African American to serve on the Supreme Court of the United States. Before that, he was a lawyer who argued before the Supreme Court and is known for the victory in *Brown v. Board of Education* (Maxine's family name is an homage to Justice Marshall and she uses his first name as her *nom de plume* for her underground essay)

Title IX: A law enacted in 1972 which states that "No person in the United States shall, on the basis of sex, be excluded from participation in, be denied the benefits of, or be subjected to discrimination under any education program or activity receiving Federal financial assistance ..." Interestingly, there is no mention of sports, but the law is best known for its impact on girls' athletics

Traif: non-Kosher

TV Dinners: Swanson TV Dinners ®, according to the Swanson food website, "were introduced in 1953, as American's viewed their first live color TV broadcast coast-to-coast. Ever since then, Swanson TV Dinners have been linked to television entertainment and pop culture." The TV Dinners were served in foil trays (turkey was and continues to be the most popular) and included potatoes, veggies and sometimes even a dessert. TV Dinners were kind of looked down upon as a lesser version of a nice home-cooked meal. TV trays were useful; a set of four or eight would would come in a carrier and then the trays unfold to a (wobbly) table the perfect size to hold a TV dinner while sitting on furniture and watching TV. They were still popular in the 1970s—my brother and I considered it a special treat to be able to whip out the TV tray and watch TV while eating dinner (probably not the best habit to get into, however ... .)

-Ville: You could stick "s" with the word "ville" onto anything and make it an adjective to make it "to the extreme." It's fun, try it! Yucksville, coolsville, stinksville . . . you get the idea

Weirdsville: weird–to the extreme; see "-Ville"

Yugoslavia: A few months after World War II ended, the new constitution of Federal People's Republic of Yugoslavia (in the Balkans, Eastern Europe), modeling the Soviet Union, established six People's Republics, an Autonomous Province, and an Autonomous District that were part of SR Serbia. They were: Socialist Republic(s) of Bosnia & Herzegovina, Croatia, Macedonia, Montenegro, Serbia, and Slovenia. Though in 1948, the country distanced itself from the Soviets, it was still a communist/socialist state and for the next fifty years suffered unrest due to ethnic tensions and eventual economic crisis. In the 1990s and 2000s, the country eventually broke up so that Yugoslavia as it was known, ceased to exist. Due to fighting in the 1990s, there were 250,000 Serbian and other refugees.

Warriors Don't Cry: A Searing Memoir of the Battle to Integrate Little Rock's Central High by Melba Pattillo Beals - This is the inspiring true story of Melba Beals, who, with 8 other African American kids, integrated Central High in Little Rock, AR in 1957

Girl Sleuth: Nancy Drew and the Women Who Created Her by Melanie Rehak - The interesting true story of creating Nancy Drew

Doris Day – Her Own Story Doris Day autobiograhy as related to A. E. Hotchner - You'll understand why Judy idolizes her so much when you read this!

No Ordinary Time: Franklin and Eleanor Roosevelt: The Home Front in World War II by Doris Kearns Goodwin - A hefty book, but a great resource for history in the 1930s through the 1950s and a good way to find out more about Eleanor Roosevelt

http://www.fiftiesweb.com/ - A fun resource to check out for fifties slang, fashion and trends

www.YouTube.com - Search for and watch "I Love Lucy - Vitameatavegamin" the next time you need to smile!

Bᴇ ᴋᴇᴘᴛ ɪɴ ᴏʀʙɪᴛ, ʜᴇᴘ ᴄᴀᴛs!

* Who is Miss Boggs, really?
* What will happen with Mary, Ann and James O'Grady?
* What will Maxine's controversial essay say that gets everyone in an uproar?
* Will Judy have her heart broken by Bob Jenkins?
* Will Beverly have her moment of glory and will she get to share it with Conrad Marshall?
* Will the Fifties Chix travel back to 1955?

Find out in the rest of the Fifties Chix series!
Look for these titles:
Book 2: Keeping Secrets
Book 3 : Third Time's a Charm
Book 4 : Broken Record
Book 5 : Till the End of Time

Check out **www.FiftiesChix.com** for updates on the Fifties Chix book series, more info on your fave characters, secret diary entries, quizzes, contests and more!

Help Angela write the next books ... visit the website and find out how!

BOOK 2

1955 1960 1970 1980 *Fifties Chix* 1990 2000 2010 2020

KEEPING SECRETS

The mystery unfolds in a future linked to the past through secrets that must now be uncovered and told.

As if their quest to return home isn't challenging enough for Fifties Chix friends Mary, Ann, Judy, Maxine, and Bev - they must also cope with a love triangle between Mary, Ann and James O'Grady; the unexplained disappearance of their classroom teacher; and the revealing essay Maxine writes for the school's underground newspaper. Hang on tight as the time-traveling quintet explodes through well-kept secrets to find the answers in the second book of the Fifties Chix series.

Sign up to get updates and read sneak previews of upcoming books at FiftiesChix.com